ISTANBUL

The Chandler Blake Story Continues

RJ SIMPSON

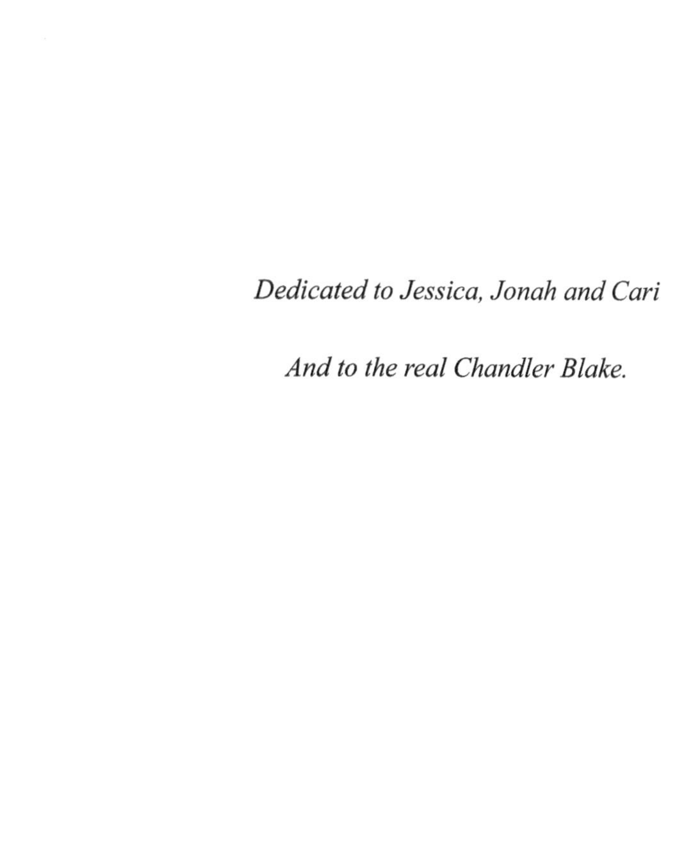

Dedicated to Jessica, Jonah and Cari

And to the real Chandler Blake.

DISCLAIMER

This book is a work of fiction.

Any similarity to persons living or dead is purely a coincidence.

ISTANBUL

Istanbul

The Chandler Blake Story

CHAPTER ONE

"3-A?" He asked, a winsome smile on his boyish face, as he stowed his carryon in the overhead storage bin.

You've got to be kidding, Chelsea Simmons thought as she shook her head in disbelief.

"This is not 3-A?" He was surprised by what he assumed was her reply to his question. He knew perfectly well this was his seat.

"The row number is directly in front of your eyes. A is the window seat." She answered none-to-politely, while trying to not roll her eyes at the absurdity of the situation.

"I see that. I just had to ask to be sure. I don't usually get a seat mate who looks like you." His enthusiasm was way over the top. "Most of the time I end up with a talkative senior citizen who wants to show me pictures of the grand-children. Or the dogs." He laughed. "Guess my luck is changing… a gorgeous woman to keep me company all the way across the Atlantic Ocean. Wow. Can't ask for more than that." His smile had turned slightly suggestive as he prattled on.

She didn't bother to respond. These guys must be getting

really desperate if they are actually making contact, she mused. She turned her attention back to the task at hand---setting her iPhone to Airplane Mode, all the while silently wondering if the ISB cloned these replicants.

He was medium height, average weight, light-brown hair, clean-shaven. This one was almost a carrot top. Just a slight hint of orange tint to his bowl cut hair. He had a few freckles scattered across his cheeks and nose. He looked like an overgrown frat boy. Come to think about it, they all looked like overgrown frat boys.

There were a few subtle distinctions… nose, jawline, eye shape, facial bone structure differentiated one from the other, but the similarities vastly outweighed those differences. Good old boys, All-American guys. Every one of them. This one fit the part, perfectly. All the way down to his navy blue, off-brand, polo-style shirt, and khakis. There was nothing that would make him stand out in a crowd. He was nondescript in every way. He would be forgotten five seconds after he was out of view. Or so they thought.

She wouldn't forget him, though. In a month, or two, when he rotated around to her, again, she would recognize him immediately. She was on to them. Totally. And she wasn't at all sure whether to laugh at their naivete, or scowl at their presumption that she could be so easily fooled. Damned idiots weren't fooling anyone but themselves. She had been on to them almost from the beginning. At this point, it was as if they wore neon signs announcing their true identity.

Nine long months she had dealt with their continuous surveillance, and in that time, she had learned to look for the least interesting person in the immediate vicinity… that would be him…. every time… it had become a game with her… a game she always won… a game she despised.

She had first noticed this one in the Medgar Wiley Evers

International Airport in Jackson, Mississippi. She was waiting to board her flight. He took his seat across from her in the passenger waiting area, casually pulled out a book, and appeared to read until time to get on the jet to Atlanta. When they boarded the plane, he sat in economy class, out of her sight, for the hour and one-half flight, and she had not seen him during her three-hour layover in Atlanta. But she knew he was nearby. She knew she would see him, again. And she was right… again. Here he was… upgraded to First Class… and it appeared he was going to be her seat mate as they crossed the Atlantic.

Now, that was new, different. Not the typical agent behavior that she had observed. Had the agency decided to up their game, or was this guy going rogue? She had no way of knowing but found the change in tactics intriguing.

Usually they kept their distance; didn't speak at all unless she forced the issue, which she had done several times, recently. Another game. This one she had initiated. Approach them. Ask a question. Any question. The more inane, the better.

"Excuse me sir, do you happen to know where I could find something that removes blood stains from the trunk of a car?" She had asked a man following her in a supermarket.

"You don't know where I could score some cocaine?" she asked a guy on the street.

They were always shaken. She could see it in their eyes, although some were better than others at hiding it. But none of them had any idea how to handle that situation. Their reactions were funny. And, at the same time, not funny at all.

They didn't like being approached. And she loved making them uncomfortable. One of the few joys she got from this untenable situation. But now it seemed as if they were possibly trying to turn the tables.

Maybe he thought, if he sat with her, it would shake her. She chuckled to herself. Not likely. With everything she had been through in the last year, it would take more than an ambitious ISB agent to upset her. He might think he could change the dynamics … well, he would regret that. She would make sure of it. The question was…how?

She toyed momentarily with the idea of playing with him. Coming on to him. Sexually harassing him, even. "Meet me in the bathroom and I'll initiate you into the mile-high club." She could imagine the faces of the people at HQ reading that in whatever report he might file. That would undoubtedly shake things up; give the people who had followed her for almost a year something to talk about. There was just not quite enough Mata-Hari in her to pull it off. He might take her up on the offer and… no… she couldn't do that, couldn't take it that far. She was a one-man woman… and this cretin, his clones, and the people they all worked for, were responsible for her not being with that one man.

"I have the window seat but if you would like to change…." He continued, still smiling. It was a nice smile. An engaging smile. One might even call it a charming smile, but, as he spoke, she had the distinct impression he was trying to fake a southern accent which would have been a complete turn-off, even if she didn't know who he was.

"I prefer the aisle…" Her voice was cool, crisp, bitchy.

"OK." He held up his hands in surrender. "I just know women usually like the window. Just trying to be polite."

"Actually, women usually like for men to not generalize about what women usually like." She snapped. No reason to pussy-foot around the matter. If he thought he was going to make small talk, lull her into some sense of false security where she slipped up and gave him information, he might as well know, from the beginning, it wasn't happening. If he wanted to play games, they'd play games, but they would be games where she made the rules. And, honestly, on second thought, she wasn't in the mood to play with him. She had grown tired of the whole thing. Right now, at this moment, she felt confrontational. Maybe, it was time.

"Point taken." He smiled, stepped over her knees that she turned only so slightly to allow him access to his seat.

"Look, I'm sorry. Didn't mean to…" he began after taking his seat.

"Shhhhh!" Chelsea shushed him, gesturing to the Flight Attendant at the front of the plane who had begun her safety in the air speech. The plane began to taxi away from the terminal, toward the runway as he continued to talk, although his tone was more hushed.

"I'm sorry, Hun. Didn't mean to generalize about women. I know you gals are hyper-sensitive about your independence these days. I'm not a sexist, I promise. I'm just really kind of socially awkward around beautiful women, and when I saw that I was sitting next to someone as pretty as you…" he began as the plane was accelerating down the runway.

Gals? Did he just call her a gal? Enough, loser. You chose to initiate contact. So, let's just get down to it. "Oh, good grief…knock it off, already. I know who you are, and I'm not interested in pretending otherwise. Ok?" She responded rudely. This had gone on long enough. She was tired of playing cat and mouse. Tired of being spied on. She had considered the idea of a face-to-face confrontation for a while, now. It was finally time to do it.

"You know who I am? I don't know what you're talking about?" he scratched his head, he actually scratched his head, in feigned confusion. "Who am I? You must have me confused with…"

"I don't have anything confused, asshole. Ok? Look…

Agent.... I'm sorry, I don't know your name. I just know Agent goes in front of it. Care to share or should I just call you ISB Robot # 17." She laughed as he grimaced at her calling out those oh so top-secret letters.

"Ma'am, I really don't know what you're talking about...."

"ISB. I'm talking about the ISB. The International Security Bureau. The deep state, undercover international investigation agency that flies under the radar where they can do all the nasty things that the FBI and CIA and other better-known agencies can't do. I know all about it, and I know you're one of their agents. Don't even bother to deny it." She rolled her eyes expressively. "Do you really think after a year of stalking me, I can't pick you guys out of a crowd?" Her voice was getting louder with each word.

"Knock it off, Chelsea." The southern accent was gone. His congenial smile had been replaced by an angry scowl.

"Chelsea? You know my name? And you admit it. Good. We are making progress. I can't imagine why you decided to make contact today, but since you did... let's make some ground rules. First, don't you dare say you don't know what I'm talking about, or I'll scream ISB so loud that they can hear me all the way back to the economy bathrooms..."

She had lowered her voice to barely above a whisper. "Now, let me explain something to you... I'm sure you thought it was a good idea, a great idea, to sit with me for the next seven hours. I bet you thought you could fake a southern accent, flirt a little, and I'd sing like a canary. You thought you could charm me into telling you whatever the hell you guys think I know. There's only one problem. Well, two, actually. First, you aren't that charming. I'm sorry but you really don't measure up to my last guy. And second, I hate to break this to you. I don't have anything you guys want. Chandler did not leave me with some top-secret package, or a safe-deposit box key, or anything like that. He didn't leave anything that incriminated you guys in anyway. Not to me. And, just so you know, he was a good agent and he told me nothing. Well, nothing except that he was in a top-secret agency that wouldn't let him out. He said there was only one exit…death. I didn't understand what he meant. But he sent me home and he took his out. Death. By Suicide." Her body shuddered as she said the word. She still could not deal with the subterfuge that he had undertaken. Could not deal with the subterfuge that she had supported.

"You guys literally harassed him into killing himself. And you've been following me every day since." He raised his eyes questioningly. Seemingly surprised by her comment.

"I hope you weren't foolish enough to think I did not know. That's damned insulting if you did. I've always known you, or one of your agent buddies, was nearby. You camped outside my hotel room, during the time I was in LA for the funeral. You followed me back to Mississippi, afterwards. You follow me everywhere I go. I've seen you, or one of your clones, every day since. I can pick you out of a room with 10,000 people, in less than five minutes… You're not even subtle. I've known, from the beginning, I was under surveillance. I've just never known why. But I figured you weren't bothering me, and I had nothing to hide so what the hell…. If you guys want to watch me from a distance, so be it. But, sitting with me on my trip is a little bit too much. You pushed your luck too far this time, buddy, … and now you're busted. I'm stuck with you for the next seven hours, but you're stuck with me, too … So, why don't we make effective use of the time. You tell me what the hell it is you people want. Cause I don't know. I've tried to figure it out and I'm clueless. What do you want? How do I get you guys to stop following me? I'm tired of seeing you losers everywhere I go. I loved Chandler with all of my heart. And I lost him. And I need to heal from that loss. I need to heal, and I can't as long as you assholes are around to remind me of what I lost. I want you to back off. I'm tired of seeing you everywhere I go... And I always see you. I mean, you've got to be the worst damned spies in the world... because I do see you... everywhere I go."

He stared at her, a perplexed expression on his face. He shook his head as if to deny and then suddenly changed his mind. He sighed deeply.

"Fine, Chelsea. Let's put our cards on the table."

"Great.... what do you want?"

"Where is he?" his voice was low, ominous.

"Where's who?"

"Chandler? Where is he?"

"In hell if you believe what the Pope says about suicide."

"Chelsea... come on, drop it... you want to go all confrontational on me, I can do the same.... We know he's not dead. We know he's still in touch with you. So, where the hell is he?"

"You don't think he's dead?"

He sighed, again. "We know he's not dead. So, do you. I thought we were going to shoot straight here. Isn't that what you said you wanted? So, fine, then, let's be honest. He's not dead. So, where is he? France? Is that why you're going to Paris? Do you plan on meeting up with him there?"

"I wish." Chelsea laughed, bitterly. "No, sorry to break it to you, but I've almost grieved myself to death over him. I know he is dead. He died after I left him. I have to live with that for the rest of my life. And it has almost killed me. So no, I don't know he's still alive. I wish I did, but unfortunately, that's just not the case." She was lying, of course. But the whole situation was so frustrating, so painful, that tears came into her eyes, anyway.

"Is he going to meet you in Paris?"

"I'm going to London."

"And then you are going on to Paris. You made reservations at the Ritz-Carlton. Requested a special room. A room Chandler has requested in the past. You might as well drop the charade, Chelsea. You're not fooling anyone."

"I'm going to London, and then on to Paris because I need to get on with my life. As I just explained to you... weren't you listening...I need to heal. Chandler and I had planned on making this trip before he died. We were supposed to go to London for Valentin Romanov's wedding, and then on to Paris. I thought if I made the trip, it would be like a goodbye tribute. A completion of our lives together."

"You've never even been out of the country. And you expect us to believe you just decided to go continent hopping on your own? That's really not even safe for a young woman at this point in time, now is it? I mean, anything could happen to you. You could disappear and never be seen or heard from, again."

"Is that a threat?"

"Just an observation. You're not really a big risk-taker, but here you are."

"I wanted to see London and Paris. I wanted to make the trip with the love of my life but that didn't work out. So, I'm going on my own... why is that so hard to understand? And, as for being in danger... I feel safe. I mean, I know, no matter where I go, you guys are going to be close by. I figure if someone did try to mug me or whatever, you'd save me... or am I wrong about that?"

"Chelsea... where is Chandler?"

"As far as I know, he's dead. Gone." It had been nine

months and her voice still broke as she said the words. "But, if, by chance you're right… and you find him. Let me know… You won't have to waste one of your assassins on him. I'll kill him myself."

"We don't want to kill him, Chelsea. We've got the message loud and clear. He wants out. We're ready to make a deal. We will cut him loose…"

"Nice offer… it would have been even nicer if you had made it before he died."

"Chandler needs to finish his assignment. He knows that. He backed out of doing what he needed to do to close the book on a case he's worked on for ten years. Once he finishes his assignment, we'll cut him loose. No questions asked. He can live the rest of his life doing whatever he wants to do. The two of you can be together… if that's what he really wants. If that's what you really want. We won't interfere. He won't have to be on the run, anymore. He'll be free. Next time you talk to him. Tell him that."

"I'll be sure and share it with the medium at the next séance."

"Tell him." he said.

"You're certifiable." She replied, dismissively, as she took her Air Pods from her purse, popped them in her ears, and turned on the music on her iPhone. She leaned back in her seat and closed her eyes. Had she been convincing? Probably not. Chandler wasn't the suicidal type and they both knew it. He had warned her there would be a lot of doubt.

"It'll be a hard sale." Chandler told her when he first explained his plan. "Agents go through a lot of psychological evaluation. They say it's necessary to keep us sane. I don't think they really care if we are sane or not. They just want to know what's going on in our heads. They know I'm not suicidal."

"So why do it?" Chelsea asked. "If they aren't going to believe it, anyway." She knew they were in a horrible situation but when he suggested a plan which involved faking his own death, she had fought against it. There had to be a better way. There just had to be. He disagreed.

"Because they can't be one hundred percent sure. And if I stay gone long enough, they'll accept it, eventually.... Then we can go on with our lives. Our lives, together."

Together. That's all it took to convince her. One word. Together. All she wanted in life was for them to spend their lives together. It was all she had wanted from the first moment she laid eyes on him. It was all he had wanted from the moment he first laid eyes on her. They just wanted to be together. And it shouldn't be this damned hard. Why was it so damned hard?

She had met him on Hollywood Boulevard. It was love at first sight. She thought he was a homeless bum. Not someone she should really even be around, much less fall for. But the attraction was there, from the very beginning. It was strong. Intense. Palpable. And as the days turned into weeks, it intensified.

He told her his name was Shiloh. The fake name he used as an undercover agent. She had written Shiloh on her office desk pad at least a million times in the weeks before she learned the truth. She was completely, totally, irrevocably in love with him before she discovered that everything she knew about him was a lie. And although she tried, afterwards, she couldn't stay angry with him. He was the man she loved, regardless of his name. Regardless of the danger in his life. She loved him. She would always love him.

She sighed deeply. In the time that had since passed by, it had occurred to her, on more than one occasion, that the homeless bum she believed him to be, would have been easier to deal with than the undercover agent that he actually was. You can walk away from the streets. Walking away from a deep state spy agency was not quite as easy. She was beginning to think it was damned impossible.

Chelsea and her flight mate did not speak, again. She listened to a book for a while. It was getting late and, with a couple of glasses of wine, she relaxed into her first-class seat, and managed to fall asleep. When she awoke, they were somewhere over the Atlantic, and her travel companion was gone. His seat remained empty for the rest of the flight. She did not see him, again.

CHAPTER TWO

She had wanted to confront her stalkers for quite some time. Felt good about finally going for it. But it probably was not the best idea she ever had. Not at the present moment, at least. She had no doubt she was still being watched. They had been relentless in their pursuit for the past nine months. They weren't going to just give up after one confrontation. She knew it could not be that easy. But, as she walked through the crowded airport, she saw no sign of the all-too-familiar archetype, anywhere.

She spent three days in England. Caught a couple of plays on the West End; took a tour bus out of town to visit Stone Henge and Stratford. She saw the Ceremony of the Key at the Tower of London, and the Changing of the Guard at Buckingham Palace; had high tea at the Savoy Hotel, where she was staying, spent an afternoon shopping at Harrods. Still no sign of the surveillance that had dogged her for nine months. It was perplexing. She had developed a sixth sense about these things, and she could feel eyes upon her. She was certain she was still being watched, so she did all that she could do to present herself as a fascinated tourist on her first trip abroad. She took pictures, bought souvenirs, listened avidly to the various tour guides giving their well-rehearsed speeches. But it was all an act, a total façade. She had never been less interested, less enthused, about anything in her life. She was merely marking time. Waiting, anxiously, for the day when she could leave the United Kingdom and be on her way to her ultimate destination.

It was a shame, really. Under normal circumstances, she would have been especially thrilled to visit Shakespeare's home. She had majored in English literature in college. It was her passion. But now, it was just one more day marked off the calendar. Three days in London. Three long days, when all she could think about was getting to Paris and being reconciled with Chandler.

On the fourth morning, it was finally time to move on, and she left the hotel early. The desk clerk had recommended a cab but, she took the tube from Charing Cross to St. Pancras Station. It was a decision she regretted immensely. Changing from the Piccadilly Line to the Northern Line at Leicester Station was a nightmare.

It was morning rush hour, wall-to-wall people. She struggled to push her way through the crowd, and down the escalator to the platform for the train that would take her on the next leg of her journey. She pulled her luggage behind her, and gingerly pushed her way past the throes of human flesh, wondering, all the while, if each person she pressed against was there to watch her.

Good grief, stop it, Chelsea, she admonished herself, on more than one occasion, as she twisted and weaved through the crowds. She was sounding paranoid, even to herself. And, she would have gladly taken on the mantle of that particular mental disorder, if it would have changed the reality of the situation. But sadly, she knew this was no delusion. She had been watched nonstop for nine months. And they were still watching. She knew it.... She knew it, dammit.... They were still watching, but for the first time, in a long time, she could not find them. And if she couldn't find them... how was she ever going to lose them? Dammit. Why did she have to out the man on the plane? Why? Why? Why? She was so tired, so frustrated with the situation that she had acted impulsively. She had not given thought to the long-term ramifications. She should have known that they would change their modus operandi once they knew she was on to them. She surely knew they weren't just going to give up.

They were there, somewhere. And she would figure it out. They weren't that smart. She had no doubt that she would once again be able to pick them out of a crowd. It wouldn't take long. But the timing was a problem. She needed to figure out who the hell was following her before she reached Paris. Otherwise, she would risk leading them to Chandler. He had gone through too much; she had gone through too much, to have it all get blown to hell now. She had to figure out who was following her. She had to know. But the question was how?

She was eager to board Eurostar and head for Paris; but she took time to browse several of the shops at St. Pancras Station, wasting over two hours in the process. She had a leisurely lunch at an Indian Restaurant, all the while looking for a familiar face. But she saw none. Finally, at two o'clock in the afternoon, she made her way to the Eurostar platform and boarded the next train.

Now she was under the English Channel, headed to Paris. Hours had passed and thus far, her shadow had not slipped up, had not revealed himself. Other than the time she spent, alone, in her condo, and the time she spent at the school where she taught, it was the longest she had gone without recognizing someone following her. It was disturbing and with each passing hour she became more nervous. She shifted positions in her red leather cushioned seat numerous times. Wrung her hands almost continuously. She had brought a book to read but she could not concentrate.

She hated seeing ISB everywhere she went. But, knowing they were there, and not seeing them, was one hundred times worse.

Her eyes darted around her train car as she assessed the other passengers. Across the aisle there was an elderly woman. She looked sweet, like someone's grandma. She was knitting a chevron design in variegated blue yarns. Nothing at all suspicious about her. Of course, there was nothing outwardly suspicious about the red-haired frat boy, either.

Two seats back, a hippie… he looked like an escapee from the 1960s…. His face was tan, wrinkled. Long black hair fell past his shoulders. He wore torn jeans, and a black tee shirt with the words *Je m'en fous,* a French vulgarity, stenciled on the front in big red letters. He had a guitar case with numerous stickers of various cities in Europe on the seat behind him, and he wore thick glasses. A possibility, she thought. But he was so obvious. They knew she would be trying to make the new tail. He was unlikely simply because he was someone who would definitely stand out in a crowd.

Near the front of the car was a family. Dad in a USA tee shirt, and knee length khaki shorts. An expensive-looking Canon camera was hanging around his neck. Mom, a red head, had probably been very pretty a few years ago. Now she looked tired, as she struggled to keep the three children under control while her husband read Frommer's Paris. Probably not one of them, she surmised. It would have been a great disguise, but the children had to be maintained. That could be a distraction. She quickly ruled the family out.

A young girl, her burgundy hair in a bob, sat near the hippie. She wore three earrings in each ear, and a nose ring. She was also reading. Chelsea studied the writing on the front of her book… not English, not French… a different alphabet. Russian, maybe? Just a guess, she had no idea, actually. But she seemed to be a possibility.

Otherwise…

Who was it? It could have been any of them, or one of the other twenty or more passengers on board. She studied each face carefully, trying to commit all of them to memory. She would probably see one of them again when she reached Paris. She might catch sight of them in the hotel lobby or following her down the street. Her bet was on the old hippie, he had arm muscles bulging through his long sleeved, waffle weave, Henley shirt. He looked like someone who could handle himself in a fight. Like Chandler. He was her bet, but she wasn't sure, and she did not like uncertainty. The enemy you don't know is far more dangerous than the one you do know. An old saying, she had heard long before she knew Chandler. Long before she had ever imagined that someday she would have enemies that she needed to elude.

She spent the entire two-hour journey people watching. It had become a pre-occupation with her. A skill she had mastered. By the time they arrived at Paris Gare du Nord, shortly after four in the afternoon, she had a story for each person on the train. Maybe she should become a writer, she mused. The stories weren't half bad.

She had fought depression for much of the last nine months and that kept her energy level low. Whatever anticipation she felt about her first trip to Paris was outweighed by her anxiety that it would end up not being what she hoped it would be. She had dreamed of visiting the City of Lights her entire life. But this was not the way she dreamed it, and she was almost despondent as she walked across the terminal, hailed a cab, and managed to eke out the proper French to give him her destination.

She was restless. Her patience was growing thin by the time they finally reached the hotel an hour and fifteen minutes later. She was an amalgamation of mixed emotions. Eager to get to the hotel. Find out what might be waiting for her there. And, at the same time, she was heartsick, worried that there would be nothing. That she had made the trip in vain.

It was apparently rush hour. The traffic had been horrible. Or maybe the traffic was always this bad. She wasn't sure, but the trip had taken longer than the guidebook had indicated it would take. She suspected the cab driver had not taken the most direct route. Looking to take advantage of the young American woman who was traveling alone.

I should have offered to double his fare for a speedy trip, she thought. Too late this time, but it was an idea she would remember in the following days, she thought, as she counted out the Euros to pay him once they arrived at the hotel. The bellboy, dressed in a long white brocade jacket, and black trousers, took her luggage from the trunk of the car and she followed him into the lobby. It was amazing. White brocade upholstery. Dark cherry-stained wood, all French provincial, which featured elaborate carvings, and the gently curved legs, elemental to the style.

She glanced around in awe as she followed the bellboy to the desk where she removed her hotel confirmation letter from her purse and handed it to the desk clerk. She had practiced asking for her room in French, but she was not in the mood to converse and, even if she had been, she felt untypically intimidated by the glamorous décor. Besides, she didn't want to waste any time. She just wanted to get to her room.

She didn't expect Chandler to be there. That would be too good to be true. But hopefully there would be a message, giving instructions on where they were to meet.

"Ms. Simmons. Welcome to Paris and the Ritz." The desk clerk said. A heavy French accent, but his English was flawless.

"You speak English?"

"But of course."

"Good. Take me to my room. Send up a bottle of champagne, a bowl of strawberries, some cheese, some croissants, and don't disturb me for twenty-four hours. I need to sleep." She instructed him, as he handed her the key card.

"Very good mademoiselle." And to her delight he followed her orders to the letter. She collapsed on the beautiful white linen bedspread in what was known as the Coco Chanel suite, as soon as she sent the smiling bellboy on his way with a good tip. After her room service was delivered, she drank a glass of champagne, stripped out of her clothes, and walked into the steamy shower in the luxurious marble and tile bathroom.

The water temperature was perfect. She had read that the warmest temperature in many French hotels was only slightly above tepid, but the Ritz was filled with luxuries and the scalding hot water was among them. She took the loofah and covered her entire body with jasmine scented bubbles and then stood directly under the ceiling showerhead, allowing the water to cascade over her, rinsing the bubbles, and her insecurities, away. She had made it. She was in Paris. And in that moment, she felt sure Chandler would be joining her.

Finished with her fragrant shower, she found a similarly scented lotion on the counter, which she massaged into her legs, her arms, her stomach, and her breasts before wrapping herself in a pink silk and lace robe she had ordered from Amazon, three months earlier… when this trip was still a dream.

After pouring herself another glass of champagne she opened the French doors that led to the balcony, and there it was… her very first view of the Eiffel Tower. It was magnificent, silhouetted against the early evening sky. For a moment she luxuriated in the beauty of the landmark, then the unbidden tears filled her eyes. Dammit. Chandler should be here. She shouldn't be experiencing this moment alone. Dammit. Where was he? Where was he?

She thought back to the night they had planned this trip. They were cuddled on the leather sofa in the living room. Naked. Wrapped in a fur throw. Their arms and legs entwined. The French doors were open revealing the roaring Pacific Ocean which came up practically to their deck when the tide rolled in. They were drinking wine, listening to music, *George Benson's Greatest Hits*, talking about their day. A fire had been crackling in the stone fireplace. And the phone rang…

"Don't answer it." Chelsea moaned, not wanting to end the perfection of the moment. But he had already picked it up, saw the Caller ID. It was a call he didn't want to let pass.

It was Valentin Romanov—-Chandler's best friend, with a request and an invitation.

"He asked me to be his best man." Chandler said, afterward, more than a little ashamed. There had been a clandestine hook-up between Chandler and Valentin's fiancée at some point before he and Chelsea had met. She didn't know the whole story. She had figured most of it out the first time she was in the room with both of them. The awkwardness so common among former lovers was apparent.

Later he had confirmed her suspicions but provided scant details and as much as she would have liked to know the specifics, she respected his reticence. It wasn't just his story to tell. He respected Sofie's privacy, he explained, as he hoped she would respect his. A little maddening for Chelsea who hated the idea in principle, but she loved his integrity too much to question it.

"All you need to know is that it happened, we both regretted it. She loves Valentin, I love you. Things worked out the way they were supposed to work out." He assured her. There was just one problem… Chandler knew what had happened between the two of them. Sofie knew. Chelsea knew. Valentin did not.

"What did you say?" Chelsea had asked.

"What could I say? He's been my best friend for 10 years. I told him I would do it. It's going to be sketchy as hell for me. Probably more so for Sofie, but what can I do?"

"How do you think Sofie will feel about this?" Chelsea asked.

"I'm sure she feels the same way I do, but she can't say anything, either. Knowing Valentin, he ran it by her before he asked me, so she gave her approval." He sighed and he was silent for several minutes, just taking it all in, and then, she remembered, his face had suddenly brightened

"You'll have to go with me." He spoke. "We'll do some sight-seeing while we are there."

Chelsea's face lit up with excitement. "London sounds wonderful. I've never been to Europe."

"Great, then it's a done deal." He eyed her speculatively. "What? Something bothering you about this?"

"No, I love the idea. I was just thinking…. London sounds wonderful, but I've dreamed of visiting Paris my entire life. We'll be close, anyway. Do you think…."

"Absolutely." He said, reading her mind. "It'll be great. We'll do London and Paris." Chandler had promised, always happy to make her happy. "We'll spend the week before the wedding in London, partying with the newlyweds, and then that night after the wedding, we'll take the Chunnel to Paris. Check in at the Ritz. There's a suite on the fourth floor. Suite 417. It has a view of the Eiffel Tower that will take your breath away. Maybe the best view in Paris." He enthused.

"Sounds wonderfully romantic." She had cuddled closer in his arms as they made their plans.

"We'll make it even more romantic. We'll open the doors to the balcony, order a bottle of champagne, some strawberries, and make love with the Eiffel Tower twinkling in the background." He promised. It was a promise he would not keep. Things fell apart just a few days later. She lost the baby she had not told him was growing inside of her. Like her, he had been heartbroken by the miscarriage, but the fact that she had kept her pregnancy a secret from him caused him additional pain. Plus, he shouldered the guilt; convinced it was because of the stress they were both under.

They couldn't wait any longer, he told her. It was time to put his plan, the horrible plan, into motion. She couldn't be there. She couldn't be part of it. She was not emotionally strong enough to handle it. Not so soon after the loss of her baby, she explained. He understood, accepted her decision and sent her home to Mississippi.

It was better that way, anyway, he reasoned. It worked into the plan. It would be harder on her in that her leaving would almost certainly cause his parents to blame her, at least partially. But, if she could handle that… it actually strengthened the story.

On the day she left… he had held her in his arms, tightly, as he whispered in her ear.

"Anniversary of the first time we made love. In Paris. At the Ritz. I'll be there. You be there too."

It had been nine long, miserable months, since that day. Nine months since she had felt his arms around her. Nine months since she had heard his voice. But finally, the day had arrived. Tomorrow was the anniversary.

Thoughts of this day were all that had kept her going… and finally it was here. She was in Paris, clinging to the hope that he would be, as well. But her anxiety was high. It had been so long, too long… with no word. What if something had happened to him? What if he didn't show up? She was confident in his love. Confident to the extent that she believed he would be there… if he could be there. He would not have forgotten. She was certain this would be as important to him as it was to her. Still, the worry plagued her. She wanted so desperately to see him. She needed to see him. Needed to be in his arms. Needed to know he was alright.

A month after he faked his death, she had gotten word via a third party… he had made it safely on the first leg of his journey. She had expected to hear additional updates, but there had been nothing. As much as she hated the intrusion on her privacy, the continuous scrutiny by the ISB had been comforting in that, she knew, as long as they were watching her, they had not intercepted him. He was still eluding them, still working on their plan to be together. She had not heard a word from him. She needed reassurance but there had been nothing but silence.

She poured herself another glass of champagne, the third, and killed it in one swallow. Then another. The fourth. Before long, she had drunk the entire bottle. She staggered around the room. Considered going out on the balcony but realized that, in her inebriated state, she might take a tumble…. She wasn't sure falling four stories would kill her, but it would certainly bang her up a bit. And she had to stay healthy.

"I'll meet you in Paris on our anniversary." She remembered the feel of his arms wrapped around her, as he whispered the words. The last time she had been in his arms. Sober, she was confident of his love, his commitment to her. Drunk, the confidence waned, and she found herself tormented with doubt. Did he remember the promise? Did he remember that it was the second anniversary of the first day they made love? Did he even remember her? Truth was, she realized, she didn't know if he would show up or not. But she made the trip anyway. She was here. Waiting on him. Hoping he was safe, alive. Hoping he had not forgotten her. Hoping that he still loved her as much as she loved him.

CHAPTER THREE

When she woke up the next morning, her mouth was dry, her head ached, the nausea all but engulfed her. She groaned out loud. Last time she would finish off a bottle of champagne on her own, forever, she thought, as she rolled out of bed, and staggered toward the bathroom, steadying herself with a hand on the wall for most of the way. Another hot shower helped, although the jasmine scented body wash that had been so enchanting the night before, now caused her to gag.

Coffee, fruit, cheese, and some hard rolls from room service helped even more. By 9:30 she was dressed for sightseeing. She felt almost human… and totally lost. Now what? she asked herself, as she surveyed her reflection in the mirror. She was thinner by fifteen, maybe twenty pounds, than she had been the last time she saw Chandler. There were a few more creases around her eyes. And, too early in her mid-twenties, she had yanked several grey hairs from her head in recent months. Anxiety was making her old before her time, and at this particular moment, she was more anxious than she had ever been.

She dressed in croppy length jeans and a lime green tee shirt which advertised a casino in Biloxi. The green was intentional. She had a matching one, color wise, when they lived in California. It was Chandler's favorite. He said it made her eyes appear even more blue. She had lost that shirt in the move back to Mississippi, but this was the same color. She bought it with this day in mind.

She was dangerously close to despair. She was in Paris. The City of Lights. It was a dream come true. There was a long list of things she wanted to see and do; float down the Seine on a dinner cruise, climb to the top of the Eiffel Tower, see the Mona Lisa in the Louvre, explore the Cathedral of Notre Dame, shop on the Champs Elysée. But she wanted to do these things with Chandler. Paris was the most romantic city in the world. Dammit. It wasn't meant to be seen alone. Dammit. Where was he?

She had studiously avoided any thought that he might not show up. You're worried about nothing she told herself when the occasional nagging doubt crept into her thoughts. Realistically, she knew, in her heart, that it was possible, but she had never believed that would happen. She had expected him to be here. She still expected him to show up. At any minute he will knock on the door, she told herself. Just be patient, he'll be here.

More pacing. An hour passed. Then, two. By noon, when he still had not arrived, she decided to go out on her own. She couldn't sit there, all day. She was in Paris. She couldn't spend the entire time in the hotel room, she told herself. She left on foot. Walked a block or two, then returned to her room. Just to make sure he had not shown up.

He was not there, and there was no indication that he had been or would be, still, she realized, it was anniversary day. She couldn't leave the hotel. She couldn't miss one moment with him if he did show up. Paris would have to wait. Instead, she spent the afternoon exploring the hotel. She took a long swim in the indoor pool. Walked around the luscious courtyard, and spent the afternoon in the Hemingway Bar, sipping wine, and talking with the bartender about the tragic life of her favorite author.

She considered dining at the luxurious Les Jardin de l'Espandun, but the idea of dining alone in the romantic restaurant with the glass domed ceiling was too depressing. She opted, instead, for an hour with the hotel masseuse.

"So tense, so very tense in your shoulders, your arms, your legs… you are like walking stress." He chided her in broken English. "You are in Paris. City of Love. City of Beauty. City of Pink Light. You should not be so stressed. Tomorrow you must go out, see the city, relax, enjoy." He was right, of course. She couldn't stay locked up in this hotel for the entire week. She needed to see the sites.

She had dinner in her room, once again. This time, she drank cola rather than anything alcoholic. Afterwards she sat on a chaise on her balcony, staring wistfully at the Eiffel Tower and wishing Chandler would magically appear. At midnight, anniversary day ended, officially, and tearfully, she made her way to bed, where she cried herself to sleep.

The next morning, she was up and dressed by nine thirty. Once again, she left the hotel on foot and this time made it to the Metro Station. She was going to see Paris… but her heart was not in it. She managed to negotiate Le Metro to the Eleventh Arrondisement, where she spent the afternoon in the Atelier des Lumières, an immersive light show featuring the works of Vincent Van Gogh. No sign of Chandler and she still had not picked out a potential ISB agent.

She sat on the floor, the sparkling lights of "Starry Night" all around her. It should have been an incredible experience.

It was almost as if she entered her favorite painting. But there was no rush of adrenalin. No thrill. The streets were crowded. The metro was crowded. But to Chelsea, it seemed as if she were the only person on planet Earth. Life was desolate. She felt totally alone… and she had never been as lonely in her life.

Later in the afternoon, she made her way to the Louvre. The line to enter through the Pyramid was insanely long, but she had read that she could also enter through the underground mall, Le Carrousel de Louvre, so, she was soon inside. She spent the rest of the day, just wandering, listlessly, from exhibit to exhibit. It was early evening when she came out. Too late to try and walk back to the hotel. She wasn't even really sure which way to go. The pink lights were beginning to twinkle. This was not smart. Not smart at all, she told herself. She was alone on the streets, after the sun had gone down. Was it safe to take the Metro back to the hotel, she wondered? Possibly, but she did not remember the name of the subway stop nearest the Ritz. She considered calling Uber. Wasn't even really sure there was an Uber in France, but she was certain that she was far too depressed to even attempt to handle public transportation in a foreign language. She flagged a cab.

She tried to fight back the tears as the cabby fought the traffic, which was, again, horrible. To make matters worse, it began to rain. Not a hard, fierce rain, but a slow, steady drizzle. The kind of rain that suggested snuggling by a fireplace with the man you loved.

Two full days of her trip were gone. Chandler was still a no show. She had hoped he would join her in the Louvre. Just walk up behind her, slide his arms around her waist, nuzzle her ear with his nose as he had done a million times before. But it had not happened. She had spent the afternoon alone. And, she realized, there is no alone quite as lonely as being alone in Paris.

How did this happen? How could something that had been so very right, turn out so very wrong. Their lives together had been perfect. Two years earlier, they had ridden horses in the surf of the Pacific Ocean, explored a cave that he had played in as a child, and then, drank wine on the beach, before making love for the first time. It had been, up until that point, the most romantic day of her life. Afterwards, for the next year and three months, every day had been perfect. And then it all came crashing down around her.... Now she was in Paris, alone. With no idea where Chandler might be.

She walked into the hotel. "Any messages for me?" she asked the desk clerk.

"Pardon?" he asked, a puzzled expression on his face.

"Parlez vous anglaise?"

"No." he shook his head.

"I speak English." A girl behind the desk, said, a moment later, informing her that there had been no messages left for her.

She turned to walk to the elevator, and it was then that she saw her. Catching her reflection in the floor to ceiling mirror. Grandma, the elderly woman from the ride on The Chunnel, was sitting in one of the white brocade chairs... still knitting. Chelsea began to laugh. Grandma was the ISB operative spying on her now? Seriously? Grandma?

Chelsea was laughing as she got on the elevator. The elevator operator eyed her speculatively as she continued to giggle. She was still laughing when they reached the fourth floor. She walked down the hall, inserted the keycard, walked into her room, and the laughter turned to sobs as her back slid down the door until she was sitting in the floor. She didn't even bother to open the balcony doors to view the Eiffel Tower, that night. She stripped out of her clothes, and climbed in between the silky sheets where she, once again, cried herself to sleep.

CHAPTER FOUR

The following days were the same. Her expectation, her hope was all but gone. She was still being watched. Grandma seemed to be a permanent fixture in the lobby. The ISB wasn't even trying too hard to disguise it. If she could pick a stalker out in the crowd, she had no doubt Chandler could do so as well. He would know she was being watched. He would know making contact was too dangerous. She was at the point where she no longer expected a romantic encounter, but she still held out hope that somehow, he would manage to at least, make contact.

She toured Paris. Saw almost everything she had dreamed of seeing. Walked around the city; took a barge down the Seine… in the daylight. She longed to do the night cruise but continued to hope that would be something she could share with Chandler. For the same reason she avoided the Eiffel Tower. She wanted to climb to the top and kiss him as they looked out over the city. That had been the dream. And she didn't give up on that dream, easily. He had never broken a promise to her. Never. He said he would be here. And she was now sure that he was here. Somewhere. He just hadn't been able to make contact because of grandma, but she reminded herself, he had been a good agent. He was trained in the art of moving around without being seen… maybe he would find a way. It wasn't going to work out as she had planned, as she had hoped. But, if she could just see him, just see his face, just touch him, then it would keep her going until they could try again. Surely, he would do something, she told herself.

He did not. She had been in Paris a week. It was her last day in the city. She considered extending the stay but, by this point, she was so hopeless it didn't even seem worth the effort. A deep depression had descended over her. She felt as if she were literally shrouded in a gloomy darkness. Getting out of bed was difficult, and she actually thought about not bothering. She could just order more champagne from room service, stay in the room all day, get completely plastered. Blot out the pain. It was what she wanted to do.

But she would never be in Paris, again. Of that, she was certain. The city of her dreams had turned into the city of her greatest misery. She would not be back. So, before she left, she had to see the Eiffel Tower and take a night cruise down the Seine. She had to do it. At some point in the future, when she was over the heartbreak of not seeing Chandler, she would regret not seeing all that she wanted to see. It wasn't going to be easy, but it had to be done.

It was after three that afternoon when she forced herself to get out of bed, forced herself to shower and dress. Inhale, exhale, one foot after the other, she told herself, inhale, exhale. A cabby who actually spoke English took her to the Eiffel Tower.

She could have taken the elevator to the top, probably should have. The emotional darkness weighed heavily on her as she climbed the steps. Her legs felt like lead as she slowly trudged to the pinnacle. Her spirits lifted momentarily as she stood on the observation deck, looking around the beautiful city. She had dreamed of this view for her entire life. And it was as remarkable as she had imagined it would be. For a minute, maybe two, she forgot her misery and luxuriated in the magic that is Paris, but the temporary euphoria evaporated when a young couple, obviously in love, came and stood beside her.

"Isn't it the most beautiful view you've ever seen?" the young girl asked her lover.

"The second most beautiful. Nothing I've ever seen is as beautiful as you." He answered, adoration in his eyes.

"I love you." She said as their lips met.

Chelsea turned to walk away. Taking the elevator down, she fought valiantly to hold back the tears that had been all too common during the week.

Moments later, she was in Eiffel Tower Park, walking across the way, when she decided there would be no dinner cruise on the barge. It would be one dream she closed the door on. She was sure there would be even more young lovers. And she just could not take it. She had tortured herself enough. She was going back to the hotel room, pack her bags, and drink away her misery. She was done with Paris. She glanced around the park. One final view of the Eiffel Tower and it was then, as she turned, she saw the grandma, sitting on a park bench, still knitting.

Their eyes met, and the elderly woman stood up and walked toward her.

"Excuse me, miss." She called out as Chelsea turned to walk away.

"Would you just leave me the hell alone." Chelsea screamed as she began to run. To her surprise, the elderly woman began to run as well, quickly caught up with her, wrapped one arm around her shoulder in a friendly embrace, and with the hand from the other arm, she pushed a revolver into her side.

"What are you doing?" Chelsea asked, terrified, as she struggled against the iron grip.

"Just come with me. Don't give me any trouble and no one will get hurt." She whispered, her voice younger, much stronger, than her appearance suggested.

"Let go of me. I mean it, I'll start screaming if you don't." she argued while struggling to get free.

"Not if you want to keep your pancreas, you won't." the old woman threatened. "Now just shut the hell up and come with me. Don't make me use this on you."

"I'm not going anywhere with you." Chelsea resisted, and with lightning speed, the umbrella in her hand crashed across the old woman's head, causing her to stumble and release her grip as she fell to the ground.

Chelsea turned and began to run across Eiffel Tower Park screaming the words… "She's got a gun. She's got a gun." Realizing as she did so, that most of the people, watching her with puzzled expressions, probably did not understand English. Even so, she continued to scream the words as she ran. She reached the street and jumped into a waiting cab. "Get me out of here. Now." She demanded.

"Got her." The driver said into his phone as he sped away from the curb. It was then that Chelsea noticed his face for the first time. It was the hippy from the train.

CHAPTER FIVE

Mentally, emotionally, she had been in a dark place all week. Now it seemed the darkness had overtaken her physically as well. She could see nothing. It was as if she were stumbling around, trying to find the light switch. And she hurt…. She hurt all over. She opened her eyes, the bright lights causing her to cry out. She quickly squeeze them shut again. "Where am I? What happened?" she did not expect an answer as she mouthed the words. It was a question she was asking herself. She was surprised when a deep, masculine voice responded.

"You jumped out of a moving cab. You're damned lucky to be alive. You could have been run down." An answer from the void.

She opened her eyes again, forced herself to adjust to the light, and immediately recoiled. The hippie was sitting in a straight-backed chair, beside the cot where she was lying. Her head, which ached considerably, turned from side to side as she looked around the room, hoping to find a door, an exit, even though, realistically, she knew that she was not, at that moment, physically capable of even attempting to get away.

"It's ok." The hippy said. "Don't be afraid, Chelsea. I'm not here to hurt you. I was told to protect you."

"Protect me? Who are you?" she asked as she continued to look around the room for a way to escape.

"Sam Roberts ma'am…" she eyed him suspiciously. "Agent Sam Roberts, ISB…. From what I understand, you've heard of us."

"I've heard of you." The room was small. In addition to the cot, where she was lying, there was a chair, and a table with a laptop computer on it. A huge map of Paris was on the wall adjacent to her, and on the other side of the room, one window featured a view of quite a few rooftops and in the distance, the top of the Eiffel Tower.

"Where am I? Why did you kidnap me?" she struggled to sit up but then, immediately, fell back against the pillow. Dizzy.

"I didn't kidnap you… I was keeping you under surveillance. You came and jumped into my cab."

"But the other agent tried to kidnap me. She put a gun in my side."

"She's not an agent. Well, maybe I shouldn't say that. We aren't sure who she is, actually. But she's not one of us."

"What do you mean, she's not one of you?"

"Exactly what I said. She's not an ISB agent."

"Who is she, then?"

"She goes by the name Mamie. We don't know a last name. She's not permanently affiliated with anyone. Not as far as we know. She's a contract person. In the past she has worked for an Irish crime syndicate. We believe she's also worked for Mossad, although that's never been confirmed. Can't say who she is working for now. She goes with the people who will pay her the most."

"Why would someone like that be after me?"

"Don't know. But she's been on your tail since you left Mississippi…"

"She has? I saw her a couple of days ago, in the hotel lobby, but I haven't seen her before. Except on the train. I saw her on the train too. I thought she was one of you guys."

"No. Not us. I'm surprised you even noticed her. You've been too busy looking for Chandler to pay attention to what was going on around you. You've taken some serious chances with your safety. Any ideas on why he hasn't shown up to meet you?"

"I haven't been looking for Chandler. Chandler is dead." She responded quickly. Too quickly. Her head was pounding, but even in her less than fully aware state, she knew she had to maintain the illusion.

"OK. Chandler is dead. We both know better but I'm not going to argue the point. I actually admire your determination to protect him. He doesn't deserve that kind of loyalty, but you're giving it to him so, whatever… let's talk about something else, instead. Like, maybe you need to ask yourself why an assassin is putting on a big show of trying to kidnap you in broad daylight on a busy Paris street?"

"She's an assassin?"

"Yeah… she is. A killer for hire."

"And she was trying to kill me?" Chelsea shook her head in disbelief. "Why? That doesn't make any sense. I don't understand. Why would anyone try to kill me?"

"She wasn't trying to kill you."

"You just said…."

"I said she was putting on a show of trying to kidnap you. If she had really wanted to grab you, or to kill you, you wouldn't have had a chance."

"I hit her with my umbrella…. I got away."

"She let you get away."

"How do you know?"

"I know how these people work. First of all, she wouldn't have tried to grab you in a crowd. And if, for some unimaginable reason she had done that, she would have put a needle in your side that dulled your senses to the point that you would have gone anywhere she wanted you to go without a struggle. She wasn't trying to get you. She was trying to make someone think she was trying to get you. My guess is that she thought Chandler was somewhere nearby and she was putting on a show for him. She was trying to lure him out of hiding."

"No, that's not right. You're wrong. She shot at me. I heard the sound of gunfire as I ran away."

"Chelsea, she's a highly qualified, highly effective murderer for hire. If she had been trying to kill you, you would be dead now. If she shot at you, she wouldn't have missed. She was putting on a show. I think she was trying to flush Chandler out."

"Chandler's dead." She repeated with less determination than she had stated it before.

"No, he's not Chelsea. And you know it. Chandler faked his own death to get out of the ISB. It was a bad mistake. He should have known better. He made a lot of enemies over the years. Now, he's out there, on his own, and someone has obviously figured out he's still alive.

Mamie wasn't trying to kill you. She was trying to get Chandler to come out from whatever rock he's hiding under… so she could kill him. He's in a lot of danger. And you need to tell us where he is. We can protect him. Protect both of you. We aren't going to make him stay in the ISB, but we need to find him. To make sure he's protected.

If he were caught by the wrong people, tortured, he might reveal things…. If he thought you were in danger… you think we've been watching you, trying to find out where Chandler is. That's partially right. But we've also been watching you, trying to protect you. If people figure out he's alive, they are going to come after you… just like Mamie did. You need to tell us where he is. You need to do that for your own safety and his."

"I don't know where he is. I don't know. I haven't heard from him since the night before he died. If he's alive, if he's out there somewhere, then I don't know where. I don't know where. I wish I did." She began to cry.

Sam stood up, walked across the room, and returned to the cot with a box of Kleenex that he tossed in her direction. He watched her as she dabbed at her eyes.

"I almost think I believe you." Sam replied.

"You need to believe me. I'm telling the truth."

"From what I heard he was truly in love with you. I guess if that's true then what you're saying makes a perverse kind of sense. He wouldn't want to put you in danger. He probably wouldn't tell you his location. It's what I would do for the person I love. Just disappear. It would hurt but it would be best. Chelsea, I think you're telling me the truth. You don't have a clue where he is, do you?"

She shook her head in the negative as the tears continue to flow.

"OK, let me give you a little advice and then, I'll take you back to your hotel room. You seem to be ok, but it probably wouldn't hurt if you got checked out by a doctor when you get back to the Ritz… and then tomorrow, you need to go back to the states, get on with your life.

I liked Chandler. Worked with him on several cases. He was full of himself. Brash. Arrogant. Took some big chances which actually made him a better than average agent… but he took those chances because he was reckless. And that recklessness has caught up with him. He thought he was the best agent that had ever worked for the ISB, when everyone knows I am actually the best." He grinned, sheepishly.

"But, pushing his arrogance aside, he wasn't a bad guy. And he obviously loved you. I'm sure he concluded the best thing he could do was just disappear and never contact you, again."

The words rang in her ears… *just disappear and never contact you again.* Over and over, she heard the words during the ride back to the hotel.

"I was mugged." She told the desk clerk who immediately called for the hotel doctor. The gendarme appeared shortly thereafter, and she was forced to file a false police report.

"I was coming out of the Eiffel Tower, they pushed me down and tried to steal my purse…" she explained. I fought back and when I hit them with my umbrella they ran away." She described the grandma, explaining that her voice indicated she was much younger than her appearance.

The doctor concluded there was no concussion, but she did have bruised ribs and a nasty cut on the back of her head. He prescribed a mild pain killer and sent her on her way. Her head was still pounding when she walked quietly into her room and out onto the balcony.

The Eiffel Tower was, once again, twinkling against the star-filled sky. Chelsea stared sadly at the scene. She was flying out of Paris in less than fourteen hours. This would be the last time she would ever see the amazing landmark silhouetted against the night sky.

She stood there for thirty minutes, just staring into space, daydreaming of the way she had hoped things would play out before it occurred to her that the door to the balcony had been opened. She was certain she had closed that door before she left earlier in the day.

"Chandler." She called out his name as she turned to walk

back into her room. There was no answer but, a message was waiting for her, lying on her pillow… a single white rose.

It was their private communication. He would send her twenty-three roses. And give her the twenty-fourth when he saw her. It had happened many times during the fifteen months they were together in Los Angeles. And the day she arrived home from his funeral, twenty-three white roses had been waiting on her. Here was the twenty-fourth to go with it.

She held the rose close to her nose. Breathing in the intoxicating fragrance. And then she lay down on the bed… heartbroken that he had not been able to deliver it in person. Heartbroken that he was not with her now.

At least, she told herself, at least she knew he had tried to see her. He had not forgotten her. He had tried to make their meeting. At least she knew he was still alive. Her relief was tangible. She had new hope. It had not worked out on this trip, but it would work out, eventually. He was out there, trying to make contact. He would find away.

In the future, she would think back about that moment, and be glad that she didn't know what that future held for them. Had she known it would be more than two years before she heard from him again, she would have certainly despaired.

CHAPTER SIX

"Today would have been my son's thirty-first birthday." Senator Isaiah Blake stood before the crowd of people, a sad smile on his face as he spoke.

"As a young man, his life held such promise. He was charming, charismatic, brilliant. I thought he would follow me into the Senate. I thought the world that lay before him was bright with limitless possibilities. But the trajectory of his life was changed forever by a tragic college event. Sex traffickers kidnapped a young woman, his friend. He was not involved in her kidnapping, not complicit, not responsible, not in anyway, but because of the way the events transpired, he was, briefly, a criminal suspect in the case. People he considered to be friends turned on him.

He was convicted in the eyes of public opinion, treated like a pariah. He felt responsible. And even when he was cleared, completely, that sense of responsibility weighed heavily on him. Crippled him, emotionally. He was never able to overcome his sense of remorse. The guilt crushed him.

He was changed forever... and, unable to conquer the

demons that imprisoned him in the darkness of his soul, he turned to drugs, alcohol, a multitude of women. He was always seeking solace. He went into a dark place and even though his mother, his sister, and I tried to help him… we tried so hard… but our efforts were futile. The Chandler we had known for the first eighteen years of his life was gone. He would never return. We could not reach him. We failed him. Society failed him." Senator Blake sighed despondently, looked away from the audience as he blinked back the tears.

"He was blessed that, in his final days, he found a woman he loved. A woman who loved him. It was the first happiness he had known in ten years, and for a brief time, we all thought that maybe that love would rescue him from the abyss. It was not to be. It was not to be. His demons had long since conquered him." Another pause as he composed his thoughts.

"I will be forever grateful to Chelsea Rose Simmons." He smiled at Chelsea who was standing against the wall of the crowded room where the announcement was being made.

"She was the only happiness he knew in the last ten years of his life. But, for a brief time, he was happy with her. And seeing him struggle so desperately to get himself together for the woman he loved, remembering the joy she brought to his life, comforts me on the nights when there is nothing but despair.

Unfortunately, he was too far gone by the time they met. It was too late to overcome the massive depression that had ruled him for ten years, and he died, tragically, by his own hand. He was twenty-eight years old. A life filled with promise snuffed out far too soon." Isaiah paused to dab a handkerchief toward both of his eyes.

"I can't do anything to bring back my son. I would give

my own life, to have him back, but I can't do that. He's gone. Nothing will ever fill the emptiness his loss has left in my life, in his mother's life. In the lives of everyone who loved him. All I can do, now, is make his life count. Help others avoid the despair that encompassed him. And that's what his mother and I have purposed our lives to do.

So… for that reason… Today, I am proud to announce the Chandler Blake Memorial Fund. This fund will be used to help the victims of sex-trafficking. Help people who have been impacted by this horrendous crime.

My daughter, Cameron Blake Scott, Cammie, has worked tirelessly in this effort for the last year. She will continue to spearhead the movement. Right now, as a United States Senator and as a father, I promise you… we're going to put a stop to sex trafficking in this nation… and we're going to help the people who have already been victimized."

Applause broke out. People began to stand, and Chelsea saw it as her chance. She had had enough. She couldn't take it, anymore. She quietly exited the backdoor and leaned against the wall outside. This had been worse than she had imagined it would be.

She had not wanted to attend. But there was no way to turn down the invitation, which had been more like a command performance. She had no good excuse for not being there. How could she not support the cause? It was certainly important. This was a tribute to Chandler. And it had been a nightmare from beginning to end.

Cammie, Chandler's sister, had stayed in touch. "I feel closer to Chandler when I'm talking to you. I think his spirit is with you." She had confided, early on. His parents had been less enthusiastic about maintaining contact. For a long time, they blamed her, but in recent months they had softened, reaching out to her, offering her comfort, support.

"He had gone through a lot of his trust fund." Ronnie, his mother, told her. "But we'd like for you to have access to what little is left." She offered when they extended the olive branch of forgiveness.

Chelsea realized quickly that she actually preferred their anger. Deserved their anger, in her opinion. She had helped their son convince them that he was a victim of suicide. She didn't deserve the love and devotion they suddenly wanted to lavish on her. But it came anyway. And now, she was having to deal with it.

"Are you ok?" it was Doug Cameron. Chandler's uncle. She was leaning against the wall; her face had broken out in a cold sweat. It was apparent that she wasn't ok. Not at all. And they both knew it. But she couldn't explain the real cause of her stress.

"Yeah, it just got to be a bit much." She smiled weakly. "I should be stronger than this. It's been almost three years…"

"Have you heard from him at all?" Doug interrupted.

The question was unexpected.

"What? What do you mean, heard from him? He's dead."

Doug smiled. "Chelsea, my nephew and I were extremely close. Much closer than he was with his parents. I regret that occasionally, now. Maybe if I hadn't offered him a sympathetic ear, he would have confided in them. I enjoyed our bond, and it was selfish of me. But I can't change that."

"He told me many times how supportive you always were. It meant the world to him." Chelsea replied.

"I was supportive. He got no condemnation from me. And because of that he confided in me. He shared his secrets with me."

"What are you saying? I don't understand."

"I'm saying that I know about the ISB. I know Chandler wanted out and faked his death. I know he planned on you joining him once he had established a new identity. The fact that you're still here concerns me. It makes me think something has gone wrong. Something has happened to him. And I just need to know what is going on? Have you heard from him?"

Chelsea stared at him, surprised; beyond surprised, she was, actually, shocked. She had no idea Doug knew the truth. Chandler had forgotten to mention that fact… or had he? Had Doug somehow put it together on his own? Was he fishing for information?

At one point in her life, she had been trusting, almost gullible in her belief that most people were exactly what they presented themselves to be. That had changed forever. She trusted no one now. Probably never would, again. Not completely. She was suspicious of everyone.

"I don't know what you're talking about."

Doug smiled, kindly. "I appreciate your devotion to my nephew. He chose well when he fell in love with you. I know the truth, and I know you know the truth, but I won't make you admit it. I just want you to listen to what I have to say…" He paused, dramatically, taking a deep breath before continuing…

"Chandler promised to stay in touch. He hasn't. I received a message from him almost a month after he…died. He made the first leg of his journey successfully. I haven't heard from him since. I know he was planning on you joining him within a few months of his… death. You're still in Mississippi. I hate to say this. I hate to even think it. But I've concluded that something went wrong. Horribly wrong.

I hold out some hope that you are still in touch with him, but if you are not, I am afraid we are not going to hear from him again. I think we have to face the very real possibility that he didn't make it. And I think it's time to tell his parents the truth. My sister is in a bad way. She's not healing from Chandler's death. She's spending tons of money on mediums, fortune tellers, charlatans who claim to be bringing messages from Chandler on the other side." Doug sighed as his eyes seemed to moisten considerably.

"He may be on the other side, I'm more than a little worried that is the only excuse for him not contacting us… but I don't believe he is sending her the messages she's being told that he is sending. Chelsea, he promised me he would let them know he was alive as soon as he was settled in his new identity, in his new life. I would have never agreed to this charade, otherwise. And things have not turned out the way they should have. This was not supposed to go on this long. Isaiah and Ronnie need to know the truth. I think they deserve to know the truth. I think you know that, too. I suspect that's why you had to get out of that room, away from Isaiah's speech, a few minutes ago. You feel the same guilt I feel when I see the grief they can't shed. If Chandler is gone… well, they will still grieve. But if they know the truth, if they know he did not commit suicide… it will help them both. And they both need help. This is slowly killing both of them."

Tears welled up in her eyes. There had been several times when she, too, considered the possible reasons for two years without contact. Death had also crossed her mind. A fleeting thought which she always quickly rejected. He was alive. She knew it. If he died, if his spirit left the earth, she was convinced that she would have felt it. The world would have become dimmer, duller. She would have known. She was convinced he was alive. But she had no idea what the explanation for his continued silence might be.

Doug was right. Something had gone wrong. Things had

not gone as planned… but he was alive. She knew it with as much certainty as she knew her own name. He was alive.

“I can’t….” she shook her head as the tears streamed down her cheeks. “I can’t.”

“I know. You are loyal to Chandler. I appreciate that. Isaiah and Ronnie haven’t been kind to you since his death. They are trying to do better about that now… on the advice of the psychics, Ronnie’s insisting on it.” He sighed, a long, slow, sigh that bespoke his own melancholy. “One of the psychics that Ronnie trusts has told her that Chandler’s ghost won’t communicate unless they forgive you.” He smiled sadly.

“But they weren’t good to you when this first happened. They blamed you and I know that must have been hard to take. You’re being very generous and forgiving and, for my sister’s sake, I appreciate that, immensely. You owe them nothing. No one could blame you if you completely turned your back on them. I fully understand that. But, Chelsea, she’s my sister. I love her. And… I think she needs to know the truth. I’m not sure when, or how, but I’m going to tell her that truth. I’m going to tell both of them. Soon. They both need to know. And I’ve kept this secret as long as I can. I just wanted to give you advance warning. I’m sure they’ll contact you when they find out. I wanted you to be prepared.”

“Can you just give it a few more months? Six more months? Can you do that?” She asked, tacitly admitting that everything Doug had said was true. “Just give him a little more time. Please.”

“They need to know, Chelsea.”

“Just a little more time, please.” Her voice had taken a pleading tone. She was practically begging.

“I’ll think about it, Chelsea. I think they need to be told

but I don't want to do anything that might put Chandler in danger… so I'll give it a little more consideration."

"Thank you." She replied, relieved. Telling the Blakes the truth was the right thing to do. She couldn't argue against that. But, saying that truth was the first step in admitting that he would not be back. She wasn't ready to admit that. Or accept it. She had not given up… dammit, she still had hope, even though it was growing dimmer with each passing day.

She returned to Mississippi on an afternoon flight the same day… turning off the Airplane Mode on her phone as she pulled out of the Jackson airport parking deck. Ding, ding, ding. Her notifications began to chime. Nine phone calls. Seven texts. Oh no, not already. Her mind had been on the conversation with Doug throughout the whole flight, and her first thought was that he had broken his word and shared the story. She could imagine them calling her, multiple times, becoming more enraged with each failed attempt; the messages becoming more irate with each call.

"I don't need to deal with this now." She said out loud to herself and considered waiting until she got home to listen. But she had never been one to postpone unwelcome news, so at the first red light, she once again picked up her phone.

To her surprise, the messages were all from her mother. Odd. Rather than take the time to listen to the messages, she quickly returned the call.

"Is everything ok?" she asked when her mother answered the phone.

"Sure. Why wouldn't it be?"

"Because you called me nine times in two hours. What's going on?"

"Oh, that. I had almost forgotten. You had a visitor. Said

he knew you when you lived in California. Nice looking man. Seemed intelligent. Hard to believe you knew someone like that and ended up with a heroin addict."

Chelsea sighed… it would never end. "Mom."

"Sorry. I know I'm not allowed to have any opinions on your personal life, but you're my daughter and I still don't understand how you got yourself involved in that mess. And I certainly don't understand why you want anything to do with his trashy family. I just don't know how your daddy and I went so wrong. We tried so hard to raise you with some values. I just don't know how this happened. I know you don't care what I think, but it is the way I feel, especially, when someone nice like this guy turns up, and I can see for myself that it's not like you didn't have some decent young men to choose from. I mean really Chelsea; I wonder sometimes if you were on drugs yourself when you were out there. It's the only explanation, otherwise, I don't know what you were thinking?"

"So, who was this paragon of virtue? Did he have a name?" Chelsea asked, not even trying to disguise the annoyance in her voice.

"He was a nice-looking guy. Probably not a drug addict. Why you couldn't have fallen in love with someone like that I'll never know. He is someone I would have been proud to introduce as my son-in-law. Now, it looks like I won't ever even have one."

"Mom." Exasperation creeping into Chelsea's voice.

"It's true. You're twenty-six years old. You aren't getting any younger. It's time you find a husband and stop moping around after that coward who didn't even love you enough to stay alive for you."

"Who was the man?" Chelsea asked, impatiently

"What man? Oh… him. I don't know who he was. All he

told me was that his name was Jason. I don't remember a last name. Don't know if he said it, or not. I gave him your address and told him you'd be home this afternoon. He said he was going to pop in for a visit. He could be there waiting for you now."

"You gave a total stranger my address? Mom, why would you do that?"

"He looked like a good guy. I can tell when I look at people. I've got good powers of discernment. I was almost twenty before I got married and I never dated a heroin addict."

"Great. Good for you. I'll talk to you later."

"Don't go being snippy with me, young lady. There's nothing wrong with a mother wanting her daughter to find a good husband. I'm the only one of my friends that doesn't already have grandchildren and at the rate you are going…."

"Bye mom."

"Chelsea just be nice to that guy. He didn't have on a wedding ring. I checked. He seemed like he might be a good guy for you. Since you seem to think you're too good for all the Mississippi boys, this one is from California. You know Chelsea, you're not getting any younger."

"Yeah, that's what you keep telling me." Chelsea said, disconnecting the call before her mother had a chance to reply.

It was an hour later when she arrived at her apartment complex in Meridian, Mississippi. Anxious and apprehensive about what might be waiting for her, she drove all the way through the parking lot, twice, before pulling into her assigned spot in the residential area. No sign of a California license plate, although certainly, the man, Jason, whoever that might be, could have rented a car. Two of her neighbors were standing outside, apparently involved in a deep conversation. There were a couple of kids on the tennis courts. There was no sign of anyone who looked out of place.

She sat quietly in her locked car for several minutes, carefully surveying her surroundings, before grabbing her carryon case out of the backseat of her car, waving at her neighbors, and hurrying into her two-story townhouse apartment. She locked the door behind her, dropped the bag on the floor and collapsed on the sofa. It had been a hard trip and she was tired. Emotionally drained. She was happy to be home.

Home? She wasn't sure when that happened. But this was now her home. When she moved in, two years earlier, just a few weeks after returning from the ill-fated trip to Paris, she thought it was just a temporary holding spot. Living anywhere in Violet Springs was just too oppressive. People there had known her since she was a child. They had no idea, for the most part, that her life had changed forever during her two years in California. And she couldn't explain to them why she wasn't the same young woman she had been before.

Besides, she was an adult. She needed to be independent. Out on her own. Her mom, especially, drove her insane. She wondered from time to time, how it was even possible that so much passive-aggressivity could exist in one woman.

She considered going back to California, but she had promised Chandler she would wait for him in Mississippi. And she was still holding on to the hope that she would hear from him. That, somehow, they would still end up together.

She took a job in nearby Meridian… teaching English to seventh and eighth graders. It was challenging. But she enjoyed it. And it kept her busy through the long months, as she waited for some word.

Time passed and she became quite introverted. Not really happy, but not really miserable either. Numb was the word she used to describe herself. She was numb. And the numbness increased with each passing day.

She rarely went out. She read, continuously. She started collecting old movies. Spent most of her weekends in pajamas, watching film noir and eating pizza or take out Chinese. There were many times when she would go from Friday afternoon until Monday without any contact with another human being. It wasn't normal. She wasn't normal. She was in a holding pattern. Just waiting… and waiting… and waiting. And as each day passed, each week, each month, she became less certain of what she was waiting on.

Two years since he left the rose on her bed in Paris. Two long years with no contact at all. And now Doug wanted to tell his parents the truth.

Maybe it was time to do that. Maybe it was time for her to finally accept what seemed so very obvious. Her mother was right. She wasn't getting any younger. Maybe it was time to move on. But how? How could she move on when she was still deeply in love with Chandler? How could she move on when her life consisted of hoping he would send for her?

She was deep in thought when the doorbell rang. It rang three times before she reached the door where she peeped through her peep hole before answering. A tall, thin man, balding with glasses, was standing on the other side. Was this Jason?

She didn't recognize him, not at all. She was convinced she had never seen him before, but, on second glance, he didn't look like a serial killer… not that she had any idea what a serial killer would look like…but he looked innocuous to the extent that she did not feel he presented any danger. Decision made; she tentatively opened the door.

"Chelsea." He said warmly. "You look great! How are you?"

"I'm good…." She answered. She was wary. He was so happy to see her that she was fearful he might offer her a hug. She wanted no part of that. His effusive greeting had made her suspicious. She should be able to recognize someone this happy to see her. But there was nothing even remotely familiar about his face. She did not know this man.

"You don't remember me, do you?" he looked disappointed, crestfallen.

"I'm sorry, I…."

"It's ok." He said humbly. "It happens all the time. I guess I just don't have a memorable face. I'm Jason Clymer. We took a couple of classes together when we were studying for our California teaching certificate. Remember? Dr. Banks's class. You made strawberry pies…. Best damned strawberry pie I ever ate. You used it to illustrate a behavior modification technique…."

Chelsea nodded her head indicating that yes, she did remember…. Dr. Banks, the strawberry pie. She was somewhat relieved. Those things definitely happened. She still had no recollection of Jason Clymer.

"You do remember?" he asked, a pleased expression on his face. Why burst his bubble, she thought? She smiled and nodded.

"I remember very well." Not a lie. She did remember the class.

"Good. That was a wonderful demonstration. You shared a lot of good strategies with the class that day…. I've tried to implement them into my school in the last year… I'm a principle now, by the way. Do you mind if I come in?"

She wasn't in the habit of letting strangers in her home. She rarely invited anyone into her house. But he definitely seemed to know her. She had been so much in love with Chandler at the time she was taking the class that she really wasn't aware of a lot of anything else, certainly did not pay a lot of attention to other men. Maybe Jason Clymer had just never made an impact.

"Sure, come on." She said, gesturing for him to enter. He walked into the middle of her living room, past the sofa, and stood in front of her overflowing bookshelf. "You're quite a reader, aren't you?"

"I like to read." She nodded. "I've been out of town. Just got back in a few minutes ago. I'll be glad to put some coffee on."

"No, that's fine. Your mother told me that you had gone to Washington. I thought about waiting until tomorrow, give you a chance to rest up from your trip, but I am flying out tomorrow afternoon, and I was worried that I might miss you, and it was important that I talk to you so…."

Chelsea sat down on her sofa, gesturing for him to sit in a nearby chair.

"So, what was so important?" Chelsea asked.

"I'll get right to the point. I'm the principal of The American school in Istanbul, Turkey. And I want you to come work for me."

"What?" Chelsea asked, incredulously. "

"I want you to come and work for me in Istanbul. I'd like for you to teach my teachers your behavior modification strategies. I've shared as much as I can remember but as I recall, you had a great program developed, and I need you there."

"Istanbul? Turkey? You want me to come and work in Istanbul?"

"Just for a year. I mean, if you want to stay longer, I'm sure we can find a permanent place for you… but there will be a vacancy in the English department next year. Maternity leave. So, we could slide you right in, and you could share your strategies with the others. And it would be an adventure for you. I remember you once saying you were very adventurous. Istanbul is made for you. Living there is a new adventure, every day."

"Well, first of all… Jason… they weren't my strategies. If you remember, I was sharing a book…. I think I still have the book, if you had your teachers read it, then…"

"But you explained it so well."

"Seriously?" She asked, a skeptical expression on her face. "So, you are telling me you left Istanbul and came to Mississippi, just to invite me to come and share my opinion on a book with your teachers…. I don't think so. Why don't you tell me what is really going on?"

He shrugged in an exaggerated fashion. "No big mystery here. First of all, I have family in Memphis, Tennessee. I visit the states every year during the month of June. I remembered you said you were a southern girl… I was thinking Georgia rather than Mississippi, but I looked you up on Facebook. I tried to friend you a few weeks ago. You didn't accept my request." He winced in a way that indicated he was somewhat insulted.

"I did see where it said your hometown was in Violet Springs, Mississippi…. I was in the states, so I came to see you in person…. and it's not that far from here to Memphis. So, when I finished with my family visit, I rented a car and here I am. Chelsea, I'm beyond proud of our school. I want it to be a model for American Schools around the globe. I'm trying to find the best programs, the best models, to implement into our curriculum. Your behavior mod techniques were the best I've seen. I mean, think about it. It's been over two years, and I was so impressed that I remembered you, after all this time. I'd like to have you work in my school."

"This doesn't even make sense."

"It makes sense to me. But I understand your skepticism. You seem to be the suspicious type. And I don't blame you. Girls have to be careful. You can look me up on Facebook. Or call the State Department, tell them this story, and ask for confirmation that I am who I say I am, Jason Clymer, the Chief Administrator of the American School in Istanbul. I totally understand you would want to do that, you would need to do that, before you give me your definitive answer. I mean, I'm as legit as I can be… but you have no way of knowing that, and given the state of our world… well, you never know… things aren't always as they seem."

Chelsea's eyes grew wide with amazement. "What did you just say?"

"I said you'd like Istanbul. Consider my offer. I'll be at the Holiday Inn until tomorrow at eleven. I really think you need to consider my offer. It's a good one."

"You said… things aren't always as they seem."

"Yeah… right. So, I don't blame you for questioning me. But, Chelsea, it is what it is. You can check it out. Check me out. I won't be offended. I want you to come work for a year in Istanbul. I think it's something you want to do as well." He stood up and walked to the door. "It's a big decision and I'm not giving you much time, but I have to have an answer by tomorrow at eleven. Just let me know." He closed the door behind him as Chelsea continued to sit on the sofa, the words echoing in her head.

Things are not always as they seem.

Things are not always as they seem.

They had been apart so long that sometimes she had trouble picturing his face in her mind. Sometimes she couldn't remember the sound of his voice. But at this moment, it was loud and clear. *Things are not always as they seem.*

She had known Chandler for several months, known him as Shiloh, a homeless guy who played drums on Hollywood Boulevard. She had been intrigued by his free spirit, infatuated with his beautiful smile and gorgeous green eyes.

He was hot. Ridiculously hot. But there was more to him than just his physical appearance. She felt a connection to him. The first time she saw him, it was there. And over the months, as they became pals, it intensified. She was completely in love with him before she even knew who he was, and so she was stunned, heartbroken, even, several months later when she discovered he was not at all who he had presented himself to be.

Chandler Blake was wealthy, indulged, a womanizer, a hard partier. Trouble on wheels. Way out of her league according to everyone who knew her, and thought they knew him. He was not at all like the guy on the boulevard that she had fallen for. But she soon learned, there was more to his story.

Don't judge me on what you've heard. Things aren't always as they seem, he told her, and it became a catch phrase between them. Things aren't always as they seem. Now Jason had uttered those same words and issued an invitation to Istanbul.

Was it a clue? A hint? Or just a random coincidence? Things aren't always as they seem was not an uncommon phrase. It was probably nothing more than a random comment with a special meaning for her that was unknown to Jason. That was probably all there was to it. But….

She might have been able to convince herself that it meant nothing, except for the odd circumstances. She did not remember that man. Jason. She had a better than average memory for names and faces and she was convinced she had never laid eyes on him before tonight. And not only that…

She thought back to the class that he said they were both in. She remembered that class. She remembered the professor. One of her favorites. She remembered several of her classmates. But she didn't remember him.

She remembered the class presentation he had mentioned. She remembered sitting in the floor of the beach house she shared with Chandler, working on that project, while he watched a basketball game on television. She had practiced the accompanying speech with him acting as her audience. At the time, he knew as much about her paper as she did. Would he have remembered that for three years? Would he have thought that would be a safe way to lure her to Istanbul? She had no way of knowing but maybe, just maybe, he thought things were finally safe enough for her to join him. Maybe…

She was overcome with almost a manic excitement. Tired an hour earlier, adrenaline was now pumping through her veins, making it impossible for her to stay in her seat. She paced through her townhouse, ran up and down her staircase several times.

She was trying to sort it all out in her mind. Afraid to hope, but hoping anyway… She had been so unsettled by the conversation with Doug. He thought Chandler was dead. And she saw no reason to disagree with him. But, maybe, they had jumped to the wrong conclusion. Maybe he was still out there. Maybe this was a message.

The world suddenly seemed filled with possibilities. Maybe, he had finally found a way to contact her. Maybe, maybe, maybe…. So much supposition, so much uncertainty. The chances of Chandler being behind the job offer were small at best. She knew that.

On the other hand, she thought, how many times in life does someone just turn up at your door and offer you a job in Istanbul? She would guess that was not an everyday occurrence. So, it was, at least, possible. And after all this time, she clung to that possibility.

She finally calmed down, settled down and stretched out on her bed, she opened her laptop, typed in the word Istanbul on her search engine, and spent the rest of the evening reading about the city that she had already decided would be her future home.

CHAPTER SEVEN

"The best kept secret in the world. That's all I can say. Istanbul is the best kept secret in the world." Chelsea explained in answer to a question posed by her college roommate, Alison, who still lived in Los Angeles. The best friend who had convinced her to move to LA four years earlier.

Alison still worked as a bartender; was still trying to make it as an actress; was still searching for Mr. Right. It was her birthday and the two were chatting via Skype.

"So…" she asked. "You've been in Istanbul for almost a month now? How do you like it?"

"It's wonderful." She smiled as she answered. It was true. She loved her new home. "Just what I needed. I feel like I'm living in the greatest city in the world. I feel like I'm coming back to life, again."

The city was fabulous. Beautiful. Historic. A city of diversity with its own unique flavor. Steeped in traditions from the old-world Ottoman Empire, but, at the same time, modern, bustling, and alive. She had fallen in love with Istanbul on the cab ride from the airport to the high-rise apartment building where she was to live. It immediately became her favorite city in the world. She loved everything about it."

"Wow. That is quite an endorsement. So, what's so great about it?"

Chelsea laughed. "Everything. The food, the people, the public transportation, my job. The Bosporus. Honestly, I even like the way the city smells."

"Yuk." Alison scrunched her nose in disapproval. "How does it smell?"

"Like Turkish leather, and fine cigars, and exotic spices… and it all intermingles with the smells of a typical town on a salt-water beach… it's amazing. I just walk outside every morning and inhale. I feel like I can breathe here. For the first time in three years, I can breathe."

She was ending her first month there and had not heard a word from Chandler. She hadn't given up hope. She would never give up hope. But she was beginning to think that, if the worst happened, if she never saw him again, she could go on. She was no longer just marking time. She was enjoying her life. She could be happy. She *was* happy. The move had been a good decision.

She felt as if she had freed herself from the shackles of the past. She had removed herself from the oppressiveness of her hometown and her mother's expectations. She was ready to start living again. For the first time in far too long, she felt like coming back to life was a real possibility.

The American School, where she taught middle school English, had forty faculty members. They were all friends, and they welcomed her into their school and into their lives in a way that she had never felt welcomed anywhere. She belonged.

"Americans in Istanbul are a very tight knit group of people." Stefany, an American from Oregon explained. "We are foreigners in a land with some remarkably different customs than what we are used to, so we tend to stick together. My husband says we are practically clannish."

She roomed with two other teachers, Chloe, an American from Nebraska who taught primary school, and Miranda, a Canadian, from Prince Edward Island, who taught Latin. Both agreed with the sentiment. We are North Americans a long way from home, a long way from family… so we become each other's family. We have to… to survive. Jason Clymer had arranged for Chelsea to move in with the two other teachers, and they had hit it off, immediately.

There were nights when the three would sit up all night talking or watching movies from Chelsea's vast collection of downloads. They spent many afternoons and weekends exploring the amazing city, sampling the exotic, but delicious. cuisine, shopping at the Grand Bazaar, the largest covered marketplace in the world.

Chelsea confided the story of her great love with Chandler… leaving out the ISB and the fact that his suicide had been faked. And she felt a special closeness with her two roomies after learning that both were fleeing from their own heartbreaks. Chloe's ex-husband had left her after less than a year of marriage for another man.

"I didn't want to be gay. I thought marrying a woman would help. It didn't." He explained to her.

"I never had a clue. I felt so stupid. I actually thought he loved me. And I did love him. I still love him enough that, I wouldn't want him to live a lie, to stay with me just because it was better for his career, or his family or his own expectations. I want him to be happy. But I just didn't know what to do, afterwards. I came from a small town. We were the gossip for months. I needed to escape and then I found this job. It was a Godsend. I had to get away."

Miranda had also suffered heartbreak when her childhood sweetheart left her weeks before their wedding; left her for one of her best friends. "She was supposed to be a bridesmaid in our wedding. I paid him a visit at his apartment, found her there, and was so naïve, I assumed they were planning some kind of surprise for me." She laughed bitterly. "Well, I sure got surprised." Like Chloe, Miranda also saw the escape to Istanbul as a blessing.

Sharing the pain with others who had experienced the loss of a great love was more therapeutic than she could have ever imagined. Even though she had not been totally honest, Chelsea felt herself healing in a way that she had not been able to heal before.

A Russian man, Anatole Turgenev lived across the hall from them, on the eighteenth floor of their luxury high-rise apartment in the Nisantasi District of the city. He was handsome, and charming, probably in his late 30s. A professor of history at Istanbul Arel University.

He and Chelsea became acquainted her second week in Istanbul during an elevator ride from the ground floor up. He was now a friend, often joining the girls for a late-night movie or meeting them for a drink after work.

Anatole provided an added layer of protection, in her mind. She was still careful about venturing out on her own. Istanbul was huge. The largest city she had ever seen. It occupied two continents, separated only by a waterway known as the Bosporus Strait.

She lived on the European side, ten minutes from The American School. From the terrace of their apartment, she could see the bridge that crossed the water into Asia as well as lights from buildings on the Asian continent, twinkling in the night sea.

The area where she lived, the Nisantasi District, served a mostly English-speaking population. She was amazingly comfortable there. Numerous fashion boutiques, cafes, coffee shops and bars lined the streets near her apartment. Nearby there was a luscious park with trails for casual walks and energetic runs which gave the neighborhood a small-town feel.

Within days of arrival, she felt quite safe moving around freely within the confines of that neighborhood. But she couldn't travel far, in any direction, without finding herself in areas of town where conversation as simple as where is the nearest subway station, was difficult. Having Anatole, who spoke Turkish, in addition to English and his native Russian, made city exploration much easier, and safer, and that, alone, made him a valued companion.

CHAPTER EIGHT

Chelsea had been in the city for exactly a month when she and her friends decided to venture out.

"Time for a party." Anatole announced on the one-month anniversary of her arrival in Istanbul. "We must celebrate."

Chelsea's roommates agreed. "You pick the place." They told her.

Since her arrival, she had heard several mentions, by her roommates and others at work, about a trendy night club, in the Bebek District. Bebek was another well-to-do neighborhood which had catered to the wealthy during the Ottoman Period in history. It featured some of the most stunning architecture in all of Istanbul.

The Emerald Club, the hottest night spot in the city, was a multi-storied Victorian style mansion on the banks of the Bosporus. Upscale cuisine was served on the ground floor and in the garden, behind. A pathway from that garden led to a dock where boaters could moor their boats while enjoying an evening inside the club. An American-style bar, appropriately named The American Bar occupied the second floor and featured pool tables, a small dance floor and a mechanical bull. A romantic, candlelit, piano bar on the third floor, with chaise lounge seating, offered a quieter, more laid-back experience while, on nights when weather permitted, patrons could dance the night away on the rooftop disco. Each floor offered a panoramic view of the sapphire sea. The Emerald Club was Chelsea's only choice for her first big night out in Istanbul.

Originally the event had been planned as a small affair. Miranda, Chloe, their dates, Chelsea, and Anatole… but when word got around the school, it became a bigger event with twenty-four people attending. It was a true party; and, among the guests, were Charlotte, another Canadian who worked as the school secretary, and her boyfriend, Ajax, a crew chief for Formula One race car drivers.

Anatole, a fan of Formula One racing, manipulated the seating so that, rather than sitting with Chelsea's roommates, they ended up at the end of the table, directly across from Charlotte and Ajax, and for most of the evening the immensely popular sport was the main topic of conversation.

It was a pleasant evening outside, and they were seated under a green and white striped canopy in the garden, which was luscious and resembled a tropical rain forest. First Bridge, the bridge that spanned the Bosporus between Europe and Asia, was their backdrop. A gentle rain was falling on the early autumn night. Rain clouds obliterated many of the stars that might have been in the sky, but the lights from the Asian side sparkled on the water and Chelsea felt almost as if she were in a Van Gogh painting. The evening was magical.

"Raki for everyone." Anatole announced, generously, when they were all seated…. Raki, the most popular drink in Istanbul, was strong to taste and very potent.

"It kind of makes my eyes wanna cross." Chelsea confided to Anatole after her first sip…

"Is this good or bad? I don't understand analogy." He asked, his eyes twinkling at the effect the drink was having on her.

"I don't know. It reminds me of the taste of licorice. I like licorice but… dang… I feel like I've had about ten beers." She giggled, after she finished her first drink.

By the time they had finished eating, a variety menu featuring lamb, hummus, eggplant, and calamari, she had had three drinks, and was giggling incessantly. "I think we may have to cut her off." Anatole announced when the waiter returned to the table for another order.

"I don't want to be cut-off." Chelsea declared loudly. It had been such a long time since she had gone out partying and actually enjoyed herself. She was happy, carefree. It was a good feeling. Not one she wanted to end.

"Well, let's at least go up on the roof, and dance some of this off before you drink anymore." Anatole suggested.

"Oh, leave her alone." Ajax laughed. "She's enjoying herself and she's with friends who will make sure she gets home safely. Drink as much as you want, angel." He smiled, encouragingly.

"That's what I want to do." Chelsea rambled on drunkenly. "I wanna do what Ajax said. And drink as much as she wants… I mean, as much as he wants…. I mean as much as somebody wants. Who wants it? What do they want, anyway?"

"Come on." Anatole laughed. "Let's go upstairs and dance."

"No. I wanna 'nother licorice drink." She said, her voice slurred, as she turned to wave her glass toward the bartender in the middle of the room.

She turned quickly back to face the table as a strange shiver unlike anything she had ever experienced rushed through her body. Something at the bar had startled her. But what? She looked back toward the bar, once again. She was tense, apprehensive. Her expansive, and somewhat inebriated mood instantly changed.

'Are you ok?" Anatole asked.

"Yeah… I just had this weird feeling like…. You know…. Like a grave walked over somebody." She scrunched her nose, puzzled, disturbed.

"What?"

"A grave walked over somebody… you know, that saying. Like this weird feeling like a grave walked over you."

"You mean somebody walked over your grave." Charlotte suggested.

"Yeah, that too." She joked, trying to laugh off her mistake, but the laugh was forced. It wasn't funny. There was something… she couldn't even find the words to describe it…. It was weird, cosmic, deja-vu like. Goosebumps broke out on her arms and she shivered involuntarily. She could feel eyes on her. Not eyes like those belonging to the ISB agents who had watched her for so long. This was different.

"You don't look so good, Chelsea? Are you getting sick?" Charlotte asked, concern in her eyes. "Do you need a jacket?"

"Anatole, my man, I think you're right. Sorry Chelsea, but you don't look well, at all. I think you probably do need to take a rest from the Raki." Ajax agreed.

Chelsea looked around the room. "No. I'm ok." She argued. "I just had the strangest feeling. Like, someone was watching me. I've never felt anything exactly like it." She realized she was far more sober than she had been a minute earlier. "Somebody walked over my grave." She looked around, apprehensively, again, and then shook her head vehemently as if to ward off the keen sense of mojo she was experiencing.

"You are beautiful woman. Many men are watching you, wishing they knew you. I am sure. Tonight, I am lucky man. The envy of many." Anatole gushed, putting his arm around her shoulder, rubbing her arm, supportively, as she continued to shiver.

"Thank you. And I'm over it now. I don't know… I just had a really weird sense of…something strange. Anatole you're right. I don't need to drink anymore. In fact, I think I need a cup of coffee. Maybe two."

"Great, ok. Let's go up to the third floor, the piano bar. You can relax up there, drink some coffee, sober up a bit." He promised. Concern still very evident in his eyes.

It became a group decision. Miranda, Chloe, their dates, Charlotte, and Ajax all rode the glass elevator up the side of the building to the third floor. Chelsea gazed at the incredible view of the sea for a moment before turning around to look at the restaurant and it was there, at that moment, she saw him.

The bar was crowded. Every barstool was taken, and the people standing behind those that were seated, were two to three deep in number. But he stood out. Grabbed her attention, immediately.

He was sitting, casually, at the bar, a glass in his hand. Long dark hair pulled back at the nape of the neck in a shaggy man bun. Dark eyes behind a pair of wire rim glasses. He was wearing a leather bomber jacket, a green shirt, possibly a polo, and jeans.

He had long legs, looked to be tall. Quite handsome. Not someone she had ever seen before, but there was something about him. The face was not familiar, but the body, the way he sat so comfortably on the stool, everything about his demeanor was very recognizable. Another shiver ran up and down her body as their eyes met. She knew those eyes.

"Damn, Chelsea, you are worrying me, baby." Anatole

said. "You're shaking like a leaf. Do we need to take you home."

"No, I'm fine…? I just…. I need coffee. I definitely do not want to go home." There was no way she was leaving this club until she found a way to meet the man at the bar.

"Are you sure?" Miranda asked, concern in her eyes.

"If you're getting sick, we can go home. Don't feel like you have to stay and party if you don't feel like it. It's your celebration. We go home when you are ready." Chloe promised.

"I'll be fine. And I want to stay. It's early. Anything could happen tonight, and I don't want to miss a single minute of it."

"I'm fine, I promise I'm fine." She reassured her friends for what seemed like the millionth time as she leaned back on the white leather chaise and sipped her coffee. I just had a little bit too much to drink and it threw me off my equilibrium. I felt weird. But it's over and now I'm ok.

"Yeah that's what you keep saying…. You felt weird like someone walked across your grave. But what does that mean? Do you think like you're dying?" Anatole asked. "I don't understand… you don't have grave."

Chelsea laughed. "No nothing like that. It's like… it's an American saying… it means like…." She tried to think of how she could explain this. The ISB shadow which had kept her under surveillance for almost two years had, as far as she knew, finally given up. She had not picked one out of the crowd in a long time. But during the time that was going on, she had developed almost a sixth sense about the spying. She knew when they were around. Before she saw them, she knew they were there.

This had been similar to that, but this was one hundred times, one thousand times, more intense. She had definitely felt eyes on her. Of course, she couldn't explain that to her new friends. She had given the vaguest of explanations about her situation in life. She had a boyfriend who committed suicide. It was a tragedy and she had had a grim time moving on, afterwards.

They didn't know the boyfriend had been a spy. That his suicide had been a ruse to get out of the business. They didn't know that she had been under ISB surveillance for over a year. She couldn't explain it, in that way… but she had to explain it. They were all sitting around her, concern written across their faces.

"OK, it's like this. Have you ever walked into a parking garage at night, and you're all alone, and you get this creeped out feeling like someone is watching you… or it gets dark and you are sitting in your living room watching television and you realize you haven't closed the blinds so anyone outside can see you… but you can't see them? It was one of those kinds of feelings. It was like I could feel eyes on me. And it was unnerving." She laughed.

"You guys were right. I drank too much Raki. I loved the taste, but it definitely packs a wallop. And it made me a little paranoid." She explained. "I'm fine now. I think we can go back downstairs.

"No hurry to go back." Anatole insisted. "You felt uncomfortable down there, so let's stay here. Much to do here."

"I'm really fine…. We can go back. I just got a little drunk and had a strange reaction. I feel much better now. I really do." She desperately wanted to make her way back down to the first floor to get another look at the man at the bar.

"Let's go back to our table and order dessert." She suggested just as the shadow of someone approaching from behind, passed over the white leather chaise where Chelsea was sitting.

"Jean-Luc." Ajax smiled and stood. And there it was, again. The odd sensation. Hairs standing prickly on the back of her neck, goosebumps on her arms and shoulders even before she heard the voice.

"I thought that was you." the man said. "I saw you going up in the elevator. It's been a while."

"It is so good to see you." Ajax exclaimed. "It's been a long time. Too long. How are you?" Chelsea sat, motionless, almost paralyzed, barely breathing, as she listened to the all-too-familiar voice. She had heard it a million times. Prayed a million times to hear it again. She knew that wonderful, wonderful voice. She turned her head slightly as Ajax began to make introductions. It was the man from the bar, as she was certain it would be.

"Jean-Luc Moreau, my girlfriend, Charlotte, her friends from American School, Chloe, Maranda and Chelsea. Their dates Anatole, Oliver and John." He made the introductions smoothly and politely

"Jean-Luc Moreau? Are you *the* Jean-Luc Moreau?" Oliver, Chloe's date, asked, awe in his voice. "The race car driver, Jean-Luc Moreau?"

"Guilty as charged." The man said, amusement in his voice. "More appropriately I guess you should call me the former race car driver."

"You are always race car driver. One of the greatest." Ajax spoke and then went on to explain, "Jean-Luc is the Grand Prix champion I worked with, for several years."

"Grand Prix champion? Damn. That's impressive." Anatole said.

"You quit racing?" Oliver asked. "Why?"

"I remember you. Weren't you in a bad wreck a year or so ago?" John asked

"Yes, two years ago. The wreck is actually why I gave up racing. Henri Lamonte blew a tire on the thirty-fifth lap at Nurburgring in Germany. He went into a spin and took out seven cars. I, unfortunately, bore the biggest brunt of that disaster, flipping 14 times and being hit at least once by all seven of the impacted cars." He sighed. "The price you pay for being number one. Everyone was looking to take me out."

"You were number one. Well on your way to your fifth championship." Ajax patted him, supportively on the shoulder. "But you can't complain, man. You are damned lucky to be alive." Ajax continued. "That was one of the most horrible days of my life. Man, when we got you out of that car, we all thought you were dead. Your body was just a crumpled heap. Couldn't even recognize your face, it was so bashed up. Completely unresponsive when the ambulance took you away. Didn't see how you were going to survive. What wasn't mangled was burned. We all thought you were dead."

"Damned lucky is right. I spent months bandaged from head to toe and when I was finally able to resume my life, I figured four Formula One championships were enough." Jean-Luc continued as Chelsea eyed him speculatively. Her mind racing. The things they were saying made no sense. What exactly was going on here?

The face was different but there was something about the eyes. Not the beautiful emerald shade of green that she remembered, Jean-Luc's eyes were deep brown. Almost black. Jawline was more square. He had less scruff. His hair was darker. Much darker. The body build was the same, but this man had a history that reached back before Chandler had disappeared.

Still, every fiber in her being was telling her that this was Chandler. But it couldn't be. She thought back to his original plan. He had told her he would create a new identity before he sent for her. This was not a new identity. This was an established identity. And he had said nothing about plastic surgery. This man did not have Chandler's face. Was she going crazy, she wondered? Had she longed for Chandler so long that she now was just imagining any handsome man she saw was him. This couldn't be Chandler. But then he would speak, she would hear that voice.... That amazing voice. And she had no doubts.

"It can't be him." she argued with herself. Rejecting her own conclusions. Maybe she'd just really gone round the bend, this time, she thought. She had been expecting to see him every day since she arrived in Istanbul. Actively looking for him. Maybe, the body similarities, combined with her desperate need, were causing her mind to play tricks.

She had heard of Jean-Luc Moreau. Remembered watching the wreck on the television during her layover in Atlanta... on the way home from her ill-fated trip to Paris. This was no fake identity, Chandler had invented. Jean-Luc Moreau was a bonafide celebrity. And yet, somehow, she was convinced that this, which could not be true, was.

"What do you do now?" Chelsea asked, her voice higher pitched than she intended it to be when she finally got up the nerve to speak.

"I have varied interests." He smiled, amusement in those brown eyes. "I spend a lot of time hanging out here, looking for someone to join me in a game of pool. Interested?"

"Oh yeah, definitely." She smiled, ignoring the exchange of glances between Chloe, Anatole, and Miranda.

"Are you sure you feel like it?" Miranda asked.

"I'm fine."

"You were about to pass out a few minutes ago. Now you feel like a game of pool. Are you sure?" Anatole protested. This was a wee bit awkward. He was not a romantic interest. Not as far as Chelsea was concerned. They were neighbors, and friends. She enjoyed his company, immensely, and he was her de facto date for the evening. They had spent quite a bit of time together in the past two weeks. He had accompanied her on shopping trips to the Grand Bazaar and the Egyptian Market. He had made no romantic advances toward her. And she had no romantic interest in him. She assumed he understood that their relationship was strictly platonic… but it was not something they had discussed.

To walk away from him and play pool with this oh so hot stranger might be insulting. She hoped he did not take it that way. But however,he took it, she was not going to let this moment pass. She could not let this man walk away until she satisfied herself that he was not Chandler.

"I'm good." She said, dismissively. "Lead the way." She gave Jean-Luc her brightest smile as he took her hand in his. And, once again. She knew.

It had been almost five years since he had first taken her hand. They were in Carmel. Their first date. Lunch at a rustic restaurant that resembled a fishing shack…the Moby Dick…. Afterwards they had taken a walk on the beach. He took her hand to help her over some driftwood, and he did not let go. They had spent the entire afternoon walking around the beach, talking, getting to know one another. And he had never let go.

During the almost fifteen months they were together, they held hands often. Always when they were walking, but other times as well. At night, after they had made love, as they cuddled in one another's arms, sleep beckoning, he would take her hand in his. It was often her last memory of the night. Her hand in his. It had always fit perfectly. Just as it did now.

"You almost passed out?" he asked, as he racked the balls. "What's that about?"

She shrugged. "I drank too much Raki… my first experience with the drink."

"I see."

"Yeah, I was a little woozy, and then… the strangest thing happened."

"What's that?" he smiled, as he gestured for her to take the first shot.

"I saw a ghost."

"You saw a ghost?" he repeated her words, unaffected by her declaration.

"That's what I said."

"You saw a ghost, here?" he shook his head, dismissively. "Not likely. Haven't heard anything about Emerald having any ghosts. There are several old mansions in the Bohemian section of town that are rumored to be haunted. Some even offer up haunted tours. There's one across the bridge in Asia that has a rich history of ghosts. As I recall, it belonged to the younger brother of an Ottoman sultan. His daughter died on her wedding day and supposedly she walks around the place. It's been turned into an investment bank now, but I hear young women who work there, insist on being out of the building by the time the sun goes down at night. Supposedly the bride still walks the halls…. if you're interested in ghosts…."

"I didn't say I was interested in ghosts… I said I saw one." She taunted him.

"I know what you said. And I'm telling you… there are no ghosts here."

The pool game continued for over an hour.

"You're very good." He said.

"I had an excellent teacher." She teased.

"An old lover, no doubt?"

"Good guess."

"Where is he now?" he asked as he bent over to shoot.

"In my heart and my thoughts, forever."

He stood without shooting, looking in her eyes. "Lucky guy." He seemed on the verge of saying more but, at that moment, Chelsea's friends came to watch. Anatole looked less than happy with her, and for that she was truly sorry. But there was nothing she could do, nothing she was willing to do, to correct the situation.

Finally, after midnight… Jean Paul looked at her questioningly. "I think it might be time to call it a night." He announced.

"Going home?"

"Yeah, that's the plan…. Going with me?"

"That's the plan." Chelsea said, trying to ignore the looks of shock on her friends' faces.

He smiled. "That was also part of my plan."

Chelsea took a deep breath as Jean-Luc took her cue stick and walked across the room to return it. "Thanks ever so much for the party, guys."

"Chelsea, are you sure about this? I mean, you don't even know this guy. He could be a serial killer." Charlotte cautioned in a whispered voice.

"He's not a serial killer. I know him well." Ajax chuckled. "Chelsea will be safe with him. I am sure of that. But sweetheart, I don't know what he's like now, but back when I worked with him, he was definitely a player so watch your step. Be careful." He seemed concerned as well.

"I'm always careful." Chelsea assured her friends, and

slipping her hand in Jean-Luc's, the two walked away as the others watched, their mouths gaping open with surprise.

"Can I ask you a question?" she asked as they hit the cool evening air.

"You can ask me anything?" Jean-Luc replied.

"Jean-Luc Moreau. That's French, right?"

"Yes, it is." He nodded.

"And yet you have an American accent. How did that happen?"

"My mother was American. She married my father, and after he retired… he was also in Formula One racing… and after he retired, they made their home in Hawaii. That's where I grew up. I moved to France and started racing when I was eighteen. I was raised in America, so I have an American accent."

"Well, that was convenient wasn't it?"

Jean-Paul chuckled. "Very." He said pointedly, as he opened the passenger door to a sleek, black Astin-Martin. A single white rose was lying on the red leather passenger seat.

Chelsea picked up the rose, turned to Jean-Luc and raised her eyebrows, quizzically. "Quite sure of yourself, aren't you?"

"Actually no. I wasn't sure how much evidence I was going to need to convince you…."

He walked to his side, slid in behind the steering wheel, cranked the car and pulled out on to the street as Chelsea examined the rose. "I imagine you have a million questions but before you asked any of them, I just have to know one thing?"

"What's that?" Chelsea said.

"How the hell did you recognize me?"

She laughed, out loud, as tears of joys flowed from her

eyes. “Chandler, baby. I knew you were in the room before I even saw you.”

He reached out, took her hand in his, and kissed it. “You have no idea how much I’ve missed you.”

“Me too.” She said, pulling his hand toward her lips. “Everyday…. This has been hell on earth. Three years of misery… but I don’t get it. You said you were going to create a new identity. Not steal one. What the hell happened? How the hell did it happen? It was supposed to be a few months. Meet me in Paris, you said. If we aren’t together before then. I’ll meet you in Room 417 at the Ritz, you said. I was there. I know you were, too. I know because like tonight I could sense your presence. And not that I needed any proof, but you left the last white rose on my bed. And then nothing. It’s been two damned years. What the hell happened? Where the hell have you been? Why didn’t you contact me? Where’s the real Jean-Luc? Why are you pretending to be him? What’s going on?”

The questions fired from her lips in rapid succession. None of this made any sense. And, even as she was demanding answers, she realized that, in the grand scheme of things, it didn’t matter. She was where she wanted to be. After all this time, she and Chandler were together again. She wanted answers, but the answers were not important.

“Ok, just calm down. I will explain it all. First of all, baby you gotta know, that week in Paris hurt me as much as it hurt you. It was the worst of my life.”

“Yeah, mine too.” She tried to keep the bitterness from her voice but the memories still pained her.

“I’m sorry baby. I know how hard that was on you. I watched you hitting the tourist sites and you looked so unhappy. I was there. I was there the whole time. But I couldn’t approach you. You were surrounded. It was horrible to be so close, and not to be able to reach out and touch you but… you were being tailed not only by ISB agents, but also the Cordoba Cartel was there as well. I don't know how in the hell they figured out I was still alive… but they were there. I couldn't even get close to you."

"I looked everywhere. I knew you were nearby. I knew it. But I never even caught a glimpse of you. I looked at every face on the metro. Every face in the hotel lobby. I floated down the Seine on a barge and looked at the face of every person sitting on every park bench on the riverbanks… I climbed to the top of the Eiffel Tower. I used the viewfinder to zoom in on faces down in the park…. I couldn't find you." She paused as a thought occurred to her. "Did you already have your new face then?"

"No, if I had this face, I would have been able to talk to you. I had some latex masks, that's why you didn't recognize me. But chances were good ISB was going to move in on anyone they saw you having more than a five-minute conversation with, and they would have figured out immediately I was wearing a disguise. There was never an opportunity, never a moment when you weren't being watched. Baby, I'm so sorry… Your first trip to Paris. I knew how much it meant to you and as the days passed, I could see you becoming sadder and sadder. It broke my heart."

"It broke my heart, too. And it scared me. I started worrying that maybe something had happened to you. I felt your presence, but I questioned those feelings. You can't imagine how happy I was on that last day to find that rose on my bed. I knew something was wrong, but at least I knew you were ok. I knew you were still alive"

"I love you." Chandler spoke softly.

"I love you too. I love you so much."

CHAPTER NINE

"I can't believe you live on a houseboat. Who does that?" Chelsea asked as they walked down the dock toward the large cabin cruiser that was secured in a slip at the Istanbul Marina, less than a mile from The Emerald Club.

"Actually, it's not a houseboat. It's either a cabin cruiser or a yacht, depending on how much of a snob you are."

"I'm not a snob at all. What are you talking about?"

"Some people argue that anything that floats and is over twenty-six feet in length is a yacht. Others say no, it has to be over forty feet. This one is thirty-five feet. Jean-Luc called it a yacht. His neighbor, my neighbor, now, down toward the end of the dock, he owns the biggest yacht in the marina. He calls this a cabin cruiser. I don't argue with him, although I understand the real Jean-Luc did. They didn't get along well at all."

"And he actually lives here. I mean, you live here. You don't have an apartment or anything like that. You live on the boat? I've never heard of anyone doing that."

"It's not that uncommon. As I said, he grew up in

Hawaii. He had a great love for the sea. He has a boat slip in every city that he's lived in as an adult. A couple of beach houses here and there, but he definitely preferred life on the water. I inherited it, all… from my namesake." Chandler explained.

"Le Peige un Castor?" Chelsea read the words from the side of the cabin cruiser. "What does that mean?"

"Are you sure you want to know?"

"What does it mean?"

"It's French. It means beaver trap."

"He named his boat beaver trap? Why?"

Chandler shrugged expressively and seemed almost embarrassed. "It's a phrase, well, some men refer to their homes as beaver traps if they use it as a way to seduce women."

"You're making that up."

"No, Chelsea, I'm not. Jean-Luc was quite fond of ladies… all of his boats, he has several, are named Beaver Trap… in different languages, of course, but…"

"Lovely." She rolled her eyes. "Sounds like someone I would hate."

"Probably. But, if you did, you would have been in the minority on that one. Women loved him. He seemed to get along with guys, as well. Had a lot of friends. It's been hard as hell to deal with all those friends without slipping up on something big. I've spent a lot of time wishing the guy was a damned hermit."

They stepped on board the deck and Chandler unlocked the glass doors which opened into a living room with a modern, almost futuristic decor. Sleek white sectional leather sofas, glass and chrome tables, silver plated lamps. Oddly similar to the furnishings in the house they had shared in Malibu, in another lifetime.

"You and Jean-Luc have similar taste?" she asked as she surveyed her surroundings.

"No. I did some redecorating when I moved in." he explained, taking her face into his hands, pulling her lips toward his. "You have no idea how much I have missed you."

She caressed his face, gently. He was the man she had loved for almost five years...but he had the face of a stranger. She shifted, uncomfortably, pulling away before he could kiss her.

"Something wrong?"

"You are a stranger."

"No, I'm not."

"No… you're not. But, at the same time, you are. How did this happen? Tell me… I need to know." She touched his face, again. "Why are you pretending to be Jean-Luc? How did you get his face? Where's the real Jean-Luc? Explain this to me. This was not the plan you shared with me. You said you were going to Europe. You said we'd live a quiet life. You didn't mention assuming the identity of an international celebrity. You didn't mention changing your face. You didn't mention we would be apart for three years. What happened, Chandler? I don't understand… and I need to understand."

"OK… come on… I'll explain it to you. I'll explain it all to you."

He took her hand in his, led her to a sofa where they sat down. He did not let go of her hand.

"I did just exactly what I told you I was going to do. And it all worked well. I found us a cottage by the sea… in a small fisherman's village in Italy. It was off the beaten track, not a big tourist place. We could have been happy there. I was anxious to tell you about it. Show it to you."

"So why didn't you?"

"I went to meet you in Paris. I knew immediately there

was no way it was going to work. You had at least three Cordoba operatives tailing you. Four ISB agents. And that's the one's I recognized. I had been out of ISB for over a year at that point, there were probably some I didn't see. I couldn't get to you in Paris, and I realized there was no way you were going to be able to come and live with me in Italy.... The day I left the rose on your bed was the hardest day of my entire life... when I left the rose, it was a good-bye, Chelsea. I didn't think we would ever see each other, again."

Chelsea blinked back the tears. "I'm glad I didn't know that, at the time. I didn't take it that way. Not at all. I. thought it was your way of letting me know you were there. That things were still going to work out. Later on, as the months passed, I began to think it might have been goodbye. But I never could make myself believe it.... I couldn't bear the thought that I might never see you again. I kept hoping, and praying, and waiting.... People told me I needed to move on with my life. They all thought you were dead, of course. And I think I heard those words, a million times. You need to move on with your life, Chelsea. You need to move on. But I couldn't.... I couldn't do anything but just wait."

"I'm so sorry. I hate to think about what I've put you through. I never intended for things to work out the way they did. When I first came up with this brilliant idea, it seemed like it would work, but I didn't take into account how completely determined the ISB is, and I didn't know the Cordoba Cartel were going to learn the truth as well."

"I don't understand about the Cordoba Cartel. I thought you said you never really were able to infiltrate."

"I never made it to the top levels. But I brought down a number of their low-level thugs. Somehow, they found out.... And were after revenge. They had an assassin, her name, the name she's known by, is Mamie. She was hot on your tail.

She would have killed me if I had shown my face, no doubt. I could have reversed the whole thing on her. Taken her out. But that would have been a confirmation that I was there, that I was still alive. And that would have put you in worse danger. It was an impossible situation. I've never felt as helpless in my life."

"So, everyone was after you."

"That about sums it up."

"But, I still don't understand. Jean-Luc?"

"After I left you in Paris, I consulted with a plastic surgeon… one I knew from my ISB days. I explained to him that I was in desperate need of an entirely new face. He was a physician of the variety that didn't ask many questions beyond my ability to pay. Which wasn't a problem. Jean-Luc had been in the accident just a few days before. He was dead, brain-dead, but they were keeping him alive on a life support system. I turned up at exactly the right time. "

"Why? I don't understand."

"He was killed instantaneously in the wreck. Ajax was right, tonight, when he said he thought he, I, was dead when they put him in the ambulance. He was dead. Should have been declared so the minute he reached the hospital, but there were some powerful people who needed for him to not be dead. They got to the doctors before the announcement could be made, and so, instead of dying, he was put on life-support while they looked for a solution." Chandler paused, a pensive expression on his face. "I was the solution."

"Why did they want to keep him alive? I mean, I understand not wanting him to die, but why would they pretend he was still alive?"

"Jean-Luc was involved in some things other than racing."

"What kind of things?"

"Money laundering."

"Money laundering?"

"Yeah, on a big scale. He worked for a European syndicate… there was a power struggle going on at the time. One side may have actually rigged his car to explode on impact. We're not sure about that. The other side needed for him to be alive. Call it coincidence, fate, dumb luck, I don't know… they approached the same plastic surgeon I had contacted. As I said, he was known for doing good-work and not asking a lot of questions. The syndicate was looking for someone to step into Jean-Luc's life. I was looking for a new life. We were the same approximate height. About the same weight. When I went to see the doctor, I told him what I needed, he told me about Jean-Luc… They didn't give me a lot of time to think about it. I said yes."

"So you launder money, now?" Chelsea asked, incredulously.

Chandler nodded. "Only in the broadest of terms."

"I don't understand."

"Jean-Luc had a number of bank accounts. He had close to two hundred million dollars in the accounts. According to the syndicate, none of it was his. He was remarkably successful. Made a ton of money racing cars. And doing endorsements. He was also a better than average baccarat player. A big man at the tables in Monaco. So, he had his money. A lot of his own money. Don't know how he got into this little sideline, but the two hundred million was not his. It belonged to the syndicate. He took it, banked it, and returned it to them, under the guise of legal gambling, where he suffered some huge losses, as they needed it. It was a smooth operation while he was alive. Very problematic when he died."

"How so?"

"He did not have a valid will. His parents were dead. No

siblings. No known children. The money would have been tied up in probate forever. And the syndicate would have never been able to get their hands on it. So… I kept him alive. After I recuperated, I went to Monte Carlo and Monaco. Took some huge losses."

"You lost two hundred million dollars gambling?"

"Slowly. I also made major regular withdrawals. Small increments. It took eighteen months. We couldn't move too fast or it might have attracted some attention. But eventually we were done. They got their money, I got a new face, and a new identity. About six months ago, I was notified that they had their money back. They were finished with me. Wished me good luck with the rest of my life as Jean-Luc and terminated our relationship. That's when I arranged for Jason to find you. I didn't want to bring you into my life, Jean-Luc's life, while I was involved with criminals. They told me, promised me, that once they got the money out of the accounts, that our association would be finished, and I could go on with the rest of my life, his life, but having dealt with the ISB and their lifetime contract, I wasn't sure. I didn't want to bring you into my life, again, if there was any chance this would be another case of me putting you in harm's way."

"I understand." She said, honestly. And she did. It was all finally making sense. "I didn't really know Jason in school, then"

"No."

"Does he know who you really are?"

"No."

"Why did he help you?"

"He's a good principal, good guy from all I can tell. He got into trouble. Not sure of the details but he was the victim of extortion for a number of years. About ten. Evidently, Jean-Luc bailed him out several times to the tune of about four hundred thousand dollars. He has been paying him back in small increments, ever since. A hundred here, a thousand there. Poor guy. I felt guilty taking the money from him. I told him there was a girl, a teacher, in Mississippi who had blown me off when I was younger. I wanted another chance with her but didn't want to be the pursuer. I told him I would cancel his debt if he could get you to agree to come to Istanbul and teach for a year. I remember you working on the behavior modification project… remembered you going to school to get your California certification… and I told him about it, thinking he could use that as a segue into offering you a job."

"He did… and he was convincing. Well, kind of convincing. I had a feeling he was lying, I mean, seriously, who knocks on your door and offers you a job in Istanbul? It didn't seem legit. Plus, I didn't recognize him, and I remember that class… I'm almost certain it was all women." Chelsea smiled. "But I had never given up. I always thought I would hear from you, eventually, and I thought well, maybe this is it. I needed a change, anyway. Mississippi was grating on me."

"I'm glad you waited it out, so I could find you. I was really worried you wouldn't be there."

"Did Jason tell you we were going to be at Emerald tonight?"

"Yes. I've been wanting to contact you but I thought, if anyone was still watching you, it would be better if we met in public. For the first time. He called me this afternoon and told me you were going to be at Emerald Club." He caressed her face, again. "Damn woman, I was so afraid you were going to move on before I could get things worked out. I'm so glad you waited. You just can't imagine how happy I was when he told me he had found you and convinced you to come to

Istanbul. I think that was the best day I've had in three years. The best day until today.."

"I couldn't move on. I knew I had to stay in Mississippi. I knew that's where you'd look for me. And I couldn't find anyone new…. I tried a few times. I dated several different guys. Nice guys. But I was miserable. I'd accept a date. Determined that I was going to actually make a go for it. But then, the night would come, I wouldn't want to go. I canceled out regularly and when I went, I'd sit through dinner, or the movie, or the ballgame… whatever, counting the minutes until I could go home. Praying the poor guy, whoever he was, wouldn't try to kiss me goodnight at the door. I wanted to move on. But I couldn't do it."

"Oh, baby… I'm so sorry. I know this has been hard on you. But I'm glad you waited for me."

"Me, too." Chelsea said.

He reached out, put his hand on her face, leaned in for a kiss, but once again, at the last possible moment, she pulled away. Standing up she walked across the room to stare out at the beautiful blue water that was shimmering in the moonlight.

Chandler followed her. Standing behind her, he slid his arms around her waist, pulling her back against his body. She stood silently for a minute, luxuriating in the feel of his body, pressed against hers.

"What's wrong?" he asked.

"I don't know. I've dreamed of this for so long but, I think it's just too much, too soon." She laughed. "I don't know how it is possible for something to take forever and then, when it finally happens, be too soon but… I don't know. This is just not how I imagined it. I mean, damn Chandler, you have a different face. It's you. I know it's you. I knew it the minute I saw you… But… It's not you. I want it to be you, and I know it is… but the face is throwing me."

"The different face was necessary, Chelsea. It's the only way we could be together."

"I understand that but…"

"It's not an ugly face." He teased. "Jean-Luc had women all over him for most of his life."

"I understand." She smiled indulgently. "It's a very handsome face. You're hot as hell, Chandler. As Jean-Luc, I mean. You're hot. It's not that. It's just…. I don't know how to explain it. It's just not the face of the man I love. And I need some time to adjust."

"OK. We don't have to make love tonight." He slid his nose down the side of her face, causing her breath to catch in her throat. "I just want to hold you. Can we do that? I don't want to do anything that is going to make you uncomfortable. But it's been so long… I just want to hold you. Is it too soon for that? Can I please just hold you?"

Chelsea nodded tentatively. He kissed her gently on the side of her neck, and turning her toward him, he lifted her up into his arms and carried her into the bedroom, where he laid her on a round bed with silky black sheets. Laying down beside her, he pulled her close to him. They lay quietly, spoon-style, and he stroked her hair gently until she relaxed into his arms and fell asleep.

CHAPTER TEN

Chelsea opened her eyes and looked around the room, momentarily confused. Where was she? And then the memories came rushing back.

"Chandler?" she called out his name. "Chandler." For one panic-filled moment she considered the possibility that it had all been a dream, but as she focused in on the details of the bed, the sheets, the large glass door that looked out on what was obviously a boat deck, the fear subsided. She was there. In his bed. It was no dream. It was reality. But where was he?

"Chandler." She called out, again. "Chandler, where are you?"

He walked out of the next room, presumably a bathroom, with a towel wrapped around his waist. His bare chest wet, his long hair hanging down around his shoulders. A handsome man. No doubt. An extremely handsome man with a hot, toned body. But it wasn't Chandler's face.

"You shaved your scruff?" she said, giggling.

"Yeah, I have to shave twice a day" he explained. "Otherwise, I end up with facial hair which is obviously lighter than the hair on my head. It causes a few double takes. Besides Jean-Luc wasn't a fan of facial hair, or so I'm told. Don't worry, though. It'll be back by sunset."

"Jean-Luc." Chelsea bit her lip. "That's going to take some getting used to…. What happens if I screw up and call you Chandler in public?"

"I'll be understandably insulted, because you called me by your ex's name, and you'll have to kiss me until you make me feel better about the whole thing." He laughed as he spoke.

"You have an answer for everything."

"I've had almost two years to get used to this idea. You've had eight hours. It'll get easier. I promise you."

"I hope so." She said with a sigh.

"It will. I promise." He kissed her gently on the nose as he sat down on the bed beside her. "Why don't you get up, take a shower… we'll go to your apartment and get some of your things. You can change clothes and we'll cross the bridge, go over into Asia, and eat a good lunch. There's a place I think you'll love. How do you feel about motorcycles?"

"I'm terrified of them. Why?"

He raised his eyebrows, suggestively.

"No way."

"Part of the subterfuge, Chelsea. Jean-Luc loved his bike, and he refused to date a woman who wouldn't climb on back. Said if they couldn't handle a bike ride, he was sure they couldn't handle riding him."

"You're making that up."

"No. I'm not." His eyes twinkled. "And the trip across the bridge is…."

"No. Chandler. No."

"Absolutely necessary. I'm not kidding. This is non-negotiable. The guy had some major quirks, and this was one of them. If you won't ride his bike, he won't let you ride his dick."

"Chandler!"

"Don't get all outraged with me. I didn't say it. He did. I just got stuck with it."

"He really said that? How do you know?"

"He did an interview with Salon less than a year before he died. It was a wealth of information. Another fortuitous tick of his personality. He gave a lot of interviews. Really enjoyed his celebrity. It gave me a lot of insight into who he was. Helped a lot when I was transitioning into his identity."

"Oh, good grief." She rolled her eyes in annoyance, resigned to her fate. "Will you at least drive slowly?"

"No."

Chelsea groaned. Chandler laughed.

"Take your shower." He grinned. "If you need some help scrubbing your back…"

"I'll be fine." She touched her finger to her lips and then to his. "I dread facing my roommates. They think I picked you up at a bar and we had a one-night stand. I mean, Chandler, they've only known me a month, and they've been so nice… and so supportive. I told them my fiancé died three years ago and I've had a hard time getting over it… and you know they've got to be thinking like…. What the hell kind of girl is she?"

"Don't worry. People are far less puritanical here than they are in Mississippi."

"Chloe is from Canada and Miranda is from Ohio."

"And they live in Istanbul. They'll be fine."

"I'm sure you're right… I just, well, I am who I am. I can't help it.

He grinned broadly. "Well, I hate to bring this up, but you didn't even play coy when I asked you to come home with me. You jumped right on the idea."

"A true gentleman wouldn't point that out." She laughed, gently hitting him with a pillow.

"Jean-Luc is no gentleman…" he paused, reflectively. "Come to think about it, that is one of the few things we have in common. He's as bad as I am. Might actually be worse." He smiled wickedly.

"I get the feeling you aren't hating this whole situation as much as I do."

"Truthfully… I'd rather be Chandler. That's who I am. But if I had to get a new identity, well, it could be worse. He wasn't a saint. Far from it. But it does seem that he lived by a code. He had a multitude of moral failings, but they all came from over-indulgence, not cruelty. He did a lot with charities, and good-deeds and the like. I've never heard anyone say he was intentionally mean, or ugly. He just lived in the fast lane. On and off the racetrack."

"Well, that's good, at least. I mean, good for the subterfuge because Chandler, I don't believe you could ever be intentionally cruel to anyone."

"Damn woman, you're too easy on me."

"I love you."

"I love you too." He responded as he gently touched his lips to hers. The first kiss in three years. He pulled away, held up his hands, stood up and took several steps backward.

"Sorry. I told you I'd give you space."

"Don't apologize. I liked it."

"Don't tempt me Chelsea. I'm trying to be strong."

"You're the strongest person I've ever known."

"Like I said, too easy on me." He kissed her again, then

turned to walk back into the bathroom. The smile on her face immediately faded.

"Whoa. Wait a minute." She said, very well aware that her voice had completely changed from playful and loving to disturbed, almost angry.

He recognized the tone of voice change and turned back around quickly.

"What's wrong?"

She pursed her lips… "Who the hell is Andrea?"

Chandler rolled his eyes. "Oh, that." he grimaced as he chuckled.

"Yeah, that." The name was tattooed on his left shoulder, along with three sets of extremely sensuous lips.

He walked back to the bed, sat down beside her, and took her hands in his. "I don't know who Andrea is. I promise. I have no idea."

"Just decided to get a tattoo and pulled that name out of the blue, did you?"

"No. Jean-Luc had the tattoo on his back. He was photographed, frequently, on the beach in Monaco, Costa del Sol, Portofino. Shirtless. Man had good abs and liked to show them off. When I took his identity, I inherited his tattoo."

"Is that the truth?"

"Chelsea, after all we've been through, I'm not going to start lying to you now."

"So, who is this Andrea?"

"Don't know. He did an interview with Vanity Fair a few years ago, and he was asked about the tattoo. Refused to talk about it. Said some things in life were private. Andrea was one of those things. Wouldn't even confirm or deny that she was the great love of his life. Just wouldn't talk about it, at all. I've done a lot of research on his past life. He had more women in a month than a lot of guys have in a lifetime… a lot of those romances were very high-profile. But I never found an Andrea. I don't know who the hell she was, or is…. All I do know is that, because of Andrea, I give thanks on a regular basis he was not a known exhibitionist."

"Why? What do you mean?"

"I mean, according to the coroner, the shoulder wasn't the only place on his body where he had the name Andrea tattooed."

"Where else?" she asked.

Chandler raised his eyebrows suggestively as he glanced downward.

"You don't mean…"

"Yep."

"Oh no, baby … you didn't."

"No, I didn't. We discussed it, the plastic surgeon and I, but decided it wasn't a well-known fact about Jean-Luc, so I managed to escape that fate. A small blessing for which I'm extremely thankful. But," he chuckled. "Obviously, Andrea was a hell of a woman, whoever she was."

Chelsea smiled, somewhat placated but, now that the question had come up… they had been apart for three years. He was a passionate, virile man. She had thought of this more than she wanted to when they were apart. And now that they were together, she didn't want to know the answer, in her heart she already knew… but she had to ask. It couldn't be avoided. She had to know.

"Chandler…"

He sighed, sadly, knowing what was coming. He had known this discussion would have to come up, eventually. He was not looking forward to it.

"Yes, Chelsea…"

"We were apart for three years…"

"Yes, we were."

"I went out on a few dates. People kept fixing me up with guys… and sometimes I was so bored, I went. I hated every minute of it. A few of them kissed me and…. Dang, one guy asked me once if I was frigid. There was another who was really nice. He didn't push the sex issue. We went out several times… but once he started, you know, coming on to me… I backed off cause… you know, I couldn't. I still loved you and… I couldn't. I guess I became a little bit of a hermit." She pursed her lips together.

He took her hands in his and kissed them. "I'm sorry you went through that… I am so sorry." He paused, and the expression on his face, even though it was unfamiliar confirmed what she suspected. She looked away, hoping to blink back the tears. Not wanting him to see her devastation. "And you want to know what I did while we were apart?"

"No. I don't want to know. I think I probably already know. But I have to hear it from you. I don't want to know, but I have to know."

"Well, ok…. Chelsea, I have not had any relationships since we broke up."

"You haven't? Really?"

"Really. But I'm sorry baby, there have been some women."

She nodded. It wasn't a surprise. Heartbreaking, yes. But not a surprise.

"I won't lie to you… as much as I'd like to, I'm not going to do that. There have been some women… but I never saw any of them twice." He kissed her hands again, as she fought back the tears. "And there was never a moment when I would not have preferred to be with you. Never a moment when I didn't wish I was with you." He paused, momentarily, seemingly near tears himself. "I'm sorry. Damn, how many times have I said those words in the last twelve hours. I'm sorry. It doesn't help, I know, it doesn't help at all, but it's true. I'm sorry for everything you've been through, everything you've suffered. It kills me to know how badly I've hurt you. Just kills me."

"But you have been with other women? You've had sex with other women?"

"Chelsea…."

"It's ok. I mean, no, it's not ok, but I do understand. We were apart a long time and I know… I knew before I asked." She said as the tears continued to run down her cheeks. She could no longer blink them away.

"I understand. I do. I just need to know. I need to know what happened because whatever happened is probably not as bad as what I can imagine. So… just tell me. Please. Who was she? Who were they? Where did you meet them? Did you ask them out? What did you do? Did you go out to dinner? Catch a movie? Did you take them for a ride in your helicopter? Send them roses? Did they sleep in this bed… on these sheets? I mean…"

"No baby. It wasn't like that."

"So, what was it like. Chandler? Tell me. I need to know. What was it like?"

"It was like, I'd be here, going completely stir crazy. Thinking about you. You know. Just miserable and unhappy and thinking like I couldn't stand this life another minute." Chelsea nodded. She understood that feeling very well.

"So, I'd leave. Ride around in the city for a while. Get something to eat. Eventually I'd end up at a club. I'd sit at the bar. Strike up a conversation with a woman… and go home with her."

"And you would have sex with her?"

“Yeah…we’d have sex.”

“Was the sex good?”

“Chelsea….”

“I have to know, Chandler. I don’t want to know. But I have to know.”

“No. The sex wasn’t good. It was a physical release. That’s all. It wasn’t even particularly satisfying. It was just a physical release.”

“Then what happened? Did you hold these women in your arms? Tell them they were beautiful? Tell them how great it was?”

“Chelsea….”

“I have to know.”

“Ok. No. Afterward, I’d get the hell out of there as fast as possible. I’d get up, get dressed. I’d promise to give her a call… which I never did… and I’d go home as soon as it was over… hating myself… Half the time, I didn’t even remember their names by the time I got to my bike. I couldn’t tell you now, for sure, any of their names. I think there were a couple of Cathy’s. Maybe a Denise. A Karen, here and there. I don’t know. It wasn’t important. They weren’t important. Their names didn’t matter.”

“That’s horrible.”

“I know.”

Chelsea wiped the tears from her cheeks. “You’re a complete jerk.”

“Yeah, I am. Although I doubt if any of them were sitting at home waiting for a call the next day. I said the words, but I don’t think I gave anyone any reason to believe it was anything other than what it was.”

“Did any of them sleep in this bed?”

“No. I never brought any of them here. I knew, well, I hoped, that sooner or later I would be able to bring you here. I knew we would have this conversation. I knew how you would feel if I told you any of them had been here… so, no, baby, I never brought any of them here."

"You're an asshole."

"Yeah…"

"I guess, damn, I guess I'm an asshole, too, because I'm glad you never called any of them for a second date. I'm glad you never brought any of them here. You treated them like whores, and I'm glad. I'm a bigger asshole than you because no woman should ever be happy to see a man use another woman. But I'm happy you did. I'm happy that's all it was. I am…. I'm as bad as you." She chuckled even as the flow of tears began, once again. He pulled her into his arms, held her close as he whispered into her ear.

"Chelsea, I'm not a saint. And you deserve so much more than you get with me. I know that. But I promise you, since the moment I laid eyes on you, the first time I saw you on Hollywood Boulevard, there has never been one moment when I didn't love you. There's never been anyone who I would have chosen over you. I was lonely and I did what I've always done to fight the loneliness. But you are the only woman I've wanted. Since the first moment we met. You're the only woman I've wanted."

Chelsea nodded. "I know. I feel the same way about you. This is just so damned hard."

"I wish I could have been a better man for you."

"Me, too. It's just so damned hard. I didn't expect it to be this hard. I thought, for three years, I dreamed about the time when we would finally be together again. I thought I just run into your arms, and we'd make love for about a month, and then just go on with our lives. Seamlessly. I thought it would be so easy. Just pick up where we left off… and live happily ever after."

"That's what I want us to do, baby. More than anything. That's what I want to do."

"But it's not that easy." She ran her hands through her hair in frustration. "It's not that easy. You're a different person."

"No, I'm not. I 'm the same man who loved you when we were in Los Angeles."

"No, you're not. You have a different face. And it's a handsome face," She giggled. "You know, you may actually be hotter now than you were before."

"Damn, woman. That's cold."

"It's cold but it's true. You may be hotter than you were before. But it's different. And I know it's you. I know. But it's still different. We're different, and you've been with other women…"

"Did you want me to lie to you about that?"

"No… I knew. I knew you didn't go three years without sex, Chandler. I'm not stupid. If you had lied, I would have known you were lying and that would have made it worse… but I don't think we can just pick up where we left off. Too much has happened. I thought it would be so easy, but I was wrong. And I don't think we can do it."

Chandler stiffened and was quiet for several seconds as he pondered the implication of what she was saying. "No." He finally said. "No. Chelsea. Come on. We can't just give up without even trying. We've been through too much. I think, if you would give me another chance, we could make this work. We've been apart for three years. We're finally together. You can't just walk away, you can't just say goodbye, again. Not without even trying."

"Goodbye again? What are you talking about? I don't want to say goodbye again…. Why are you saying this?"

"You said it. You said we can't get back together."

"No, I didn't. I never said that. I would never say that. I said we can't just pick up where we left off. I didn't mean we had to end it. We can't end it. I just think we are going to have to take some time. Get to know each other again. Re-establish the trust."

"Get to know each other again?" He sighed, with enormous relief. He pressed his lips hard on hers for a moment. "You scared the hell out of me. Damn woman, my heart almost stopped beating. I thought…" he paused, trying to regain his bearings. "I thought you were saying you didn't want us to be together… that you wanted to walk away. Not even give it a try."

"No. I could never say that. I just…"

"It's ok. I get it. You want to take it slow. And we can do that. We can definitely do that. Just spend time together, get to know each other again… we can do that. We can take as much time as you need. As long as we are together. I just thought…."

Chelsea touched his lips with her finger. "I would never say that. I couldn't do that even if I wanted to. I love you too much to ever walk away."

She touched his lips lightly with hers, pulled away and looked into his eyes. Even with the brown tinted contacts, the eyes were the one place she could see the man she loved. She caressed his face with her hand.

"I love you." He said. Kissing her again, pushing her back on the bed. She wrapped her arms around his shoulders, as he sprinkled kisses over her face and neck. He moaned softly as she pulled him closer to her. She arched her body toward his and then, he quickly pulled away. Off the bed again, hands up in a surrender posture, again. "Take our time. Take it easy. Right?"

"Yeah…" She said sadly.

"OK, great. That's fantastic. Just great. I'm going to get dressed and cook you some breakfast. You take your shower. I'm going to make you the best omelet you've tasted since the last time I cooked you an omelet.'

"Can't wait."

CHAPTER ELEVEN

"Home sweet home." She said, embarrassed, when she let herself into her apartment shortly after noon.

"Thank God." Miranda, who was sitting in front of the television, said. "We were so worried about you."

"Is that Chelsea?" Chloe called out from her bedroom. A minute later she was in the living room as well.

"Are you ok?" Chloe asked. "You look a little shaken up?"

"I'm fine." Chelsea smiled, weakly. "Jean-Luc has a motor bike, and we rode it from his houseboat, here. It's not my favorite form of transportation."

"I can imagine. Not with this traffic. But you're ok, otherwise?"

Chelsea nodded.

"I'm glad. After you left, we thought like, maybe we should have stopped you, somehow. You had a lot to drink, and we were afraid you were going to be like, why did you let me leave with him? I'm sorry, Chelsea. We broke girls rule number one. When we go out together, we go home together.

That way no one gets in trouble. We were just all a little starstruck, I think. Jean-Luc Moreau is an international celebrity, and we were just like…OK, you go girl, but afterwards we all felt bad."

"No…don't feel bad. I was not drunk. Well, maybe a little, but I knew exactly what I was doing." She explained. "I should be apologizing to you. I know my behavior looked … well, skanky as hell. You probably both think I'm terrible. Maybe I am. But believe it or not, going home with Jean-Luc was not a spur of the moment decision. It was a lot more thought out than you realized.

I told you my fiancé died three years ago." This was the lie she had decided would be best. "And I haven't been with a guy since. I just haven't been able to get on with my life, at all. And I need to. I know I need to move on. Coming to Istanbul was part of deciding to move on… and when I did that, I told myself the next time I met a guy I found appealing, I was just going to go for it…. Dive right in.

If it turned out to be a major mistake, then I'd deal with the ramifications, later. But I needed to get back into the act of living. So, I did. Jean-Luc was hot. He was interested. I said, OK, Chelsea, do it. And I did it. And I have no regrets. It was a lovely night.

And I certainly don't blame the two of you. In the long run, it probably was not the smartest move I've ever made, but you all knew who I was with, where I was. Ajax knew him personally and said he wouldn't hurt me… well, he wouldn't physically, at least. I felt safe… and I think it was a good thing for my emotional health. And as it turned out, he's a nice guy. I'm going to see him, again."

Chloe and Maranda exchanged glances.

"Well, I'm all about moving on with your life. But I

wouldn't count on seeing him, again, Chelsea. I think he's a bit of a rounder. Ajax said...."

What Ajax said would, forever, remain unrepeated because, just at that moment, the doorbell rang.

"That's probably. Ch---, uhm, Jean-Luc," Chelsea said.... Stumbling over the new name. That was going to take some adjustment in her mind. "He let me off in front and was looking for a place to park."

She walked quickly to the door where she found both Jean-Luc, and Anatole.

"Hello, stranger." Chandler said, flirtatiously.

"Hi." Anatole said, his eyes traveling from Chelsea to Chandler. "What's going on?"

"Well, I'm going to throw a few things in a bag and Cha —Jean-Luc is taking me over to the Asian side of the city...."

"Yeah, Chelsea mentioned she liked organic food... excellent restaurant, on the Marmara Sea. One of the best in Istanbul. A very holistic approach to cuisine. Gourmet health food."

"We are going to take his boat. It'll probably be late when we get back ... so I'm just going to grab a few things, just in case. And I'll see you two at school on Monday, if not before." She said as she retreated to her room where she hurriedly threw a couple of changes of clothing in a backpack.

When she came back into the living room, Anatole and Chandler were in a deep discussion about auto racing. Chloe grabbed her by the arm, and none too gently led her into the kitchen.

"If you need us, call us." She advised.

"I will. Thank you. But honestly, he seems like a nice guy. I think I'm fine. "

"Yes, he does, not at all like the guy Ajax described...

and I agree, Chelsea, no condemnation here at all. After three years, it's time for you to move on with your life… still---if you need us…." Chelsea smiled. It was nice to have friends who supported her decisions.

"Ready for another ride on my bike?" Chandler asked when she walked back into the room.

"As ready as I'm ever going to be." She declared, a hint of reluctance in her voice. After hugging her two friends, and Anatole, who still had a disappointed look on his face, they walked out of the apartment together… and started their new life, as a couple, in Istanbul.

CHAPTER TWELVE

"Leaving your new friends was hard on you, wasn't it?' Chandler asked as they sped across the Bosporus Strait in Jean-Luc's Silver Bullet speed boat.

"This is really a nice boat." Chelsea commented, leaning back, enjoying the sun on the crisp autumn day. "Is this yours or is it another Jean-Luc toy?"

"Jean-Luc. That guy had every toy, as you call it, known to man. I started trying to inventory it all one day and after writing for a couple of hours my hand got a cramp." He flexed his hand to illustrate his point. "He has five different motor bikes. We'll have to take a ride on each of them."

"I can hardly wait." She proclaimed, sarcastically. "What about helicopters?" That had been a great passion of Chandler's.

"Sadly, no. And I can't figure out exactly how to approach that. I'll have to take lessons, again, to get a license to operate in Jean-Luc's name and Chelsea, you're changing the subject on me.... You were sad to leave your friends, weren't you?"

She sighed. “Yeah, kind of, well, not exactly.” She vacillated.

“There’s a nice straight-forward answer.”

“You asked…”

“Tell me what you are thinking. I’ve always been able to read you, but I’m having a little trouble right now. What’s going on in your mind?”

“I don’t know. I only knew them for a month, Anatole less than that. I met him about two weeks ago. But they’ve been nice to me. And I felt bad lying to them. I mean, I threw a few things in a bag and said it was just for the weekend… see you Monday. But I’m not going back there to live. You know that. I know it. I felt deceitful. Which isn’t right when you consider how good they’ve been to me since I got here.”

“Well, Chelsea, as far as they know, we met less than twenty-four hours ago. You really couldn’t tell them we were planning on spending the rest of our lives together…”

“I know. But is still felt like I was lying to them… and then, there’s this new identity thing you’ve got going on. I mean, I don’t know how to deal with it. I stumbled all over your name when I was talking to them. I’d be surprised if they didn’t notice. I almost called you Chandler twice, and after that, I was so afraid I’d call you Chandler that I would literally pause every time I said Jean-Luc… to make sure I had it right.”

“And that’s totally understandable… and manageable. You were in a relationship with a guy named Chandler for years… now you’re starting a new relationship. You can always say something like, ‘Oh, don’t tell Jean-Luc I called him Chandler.’ Say you get us confused. And Jean-Luc probably wouldn’t like it very much… say part of the attraction is that you feel comfortable with Jean-Luc like you did with Chandler…”

"I think Jean-Luc would probably hate that."

"He would definitely hate for you to confuse him with another man… but given the circumstances, he will forgive you."

"Did you have any trouble getting used to the new name?"

"Not really. But keep in mind, I was in the hospital. The doctor and, at least, one of the nurses were on to my ruse. I was wrapped in bandages for a number of months, both because of my own plastic surgery, and because of the skin grafts and surgeries that Jean-Luc would have needed, had he survived.

They limited my visitors, claimed it was because of the possibility of infection from all the burns. The doctor told the friends that came to visit that I had suffered some brain damage and was dealing with intermittent amnesia. That helped because, when he, I, did have visitors, I could just claim I didn't remember something and most would spend as much time as the doctors would allow, telling me all about whatever I said I had forgotten.

This went on for months, and I had all those months to get used to the idea that I was now Jean-Luc. And then, I went to rehab. Which also limited visitors. And gave me plenty of time to study Jean-Luc and get used to the idea of being him. By the time I was ready to face the public I knew everything there was to know about the guy, and I was very used to the idea of being him. It just took some time.

You've had sixteen hours. You'll get used to it…. And in the meantime, it's better, like I told you, if you stay with me. Limit your interaction where you might slip up. Even if we're not totally together."

"I'm sorry. I'm just…"

"Stop apologizing. Stop being so hard on yourself. I love

you. And when we are together again, I want it to be like it was before. I want you to be as comfortable with me, as much in love with me, as you were the first time we made love. Remember that first day on the beach… you didn't have a doubt in your mind that we belonged together. I want you to feel that same way when we make love again. "

"I'll never forget that day. It was the best day of my life. Well, the first best day of my life… there were a lot of others that followed."

"I won't forget it, either… you were totally ready for us to be together. Had no reservations whatsoever. There was so much love in that moment… and that's what I want again. I want you to love me now as much as you loved me then."

"Chandler, I do love you."

"I know, baby. But you aren't comfortable with the new face, and the new name, and all the baggage that goes along with it. I understand that… and we are just going to have to take as much time as you need to make you comfortable with the whole thing, again."

"Thank you." She said, gratefully.

"Look." He gestured toward the shore. A mansion with stone walls, turrets, and steep rooflines was on the shore, immediately in front of them.

"That is the most beautiful house I've ever seen. Does someone really live there?" Chelsea asked in awe.

"No, it's the restaurant where we are going to eat." He explained. .

A moment later they pulled up to the dock and the yacht valet quickly took control of the boat, as Chandler took Chelsea's arm and helped her on to the deck. He lovingly kissed her hand as they walked on a cobblestone path into a beautiful garden with exotic, fragrant flowers and greenery blooming throughout. The stone, in the pathway through the garden, matched the stone exterior of the house. Several fountains along the way spewed beautiful rainbow-colored waters. A young Asian girl walked them to a table beside an outdoor fire pit, which provided the perfect warmth on the cool, breezy day.

They spent the afternoon drinking tea and trying a variety of vegetarian appetizers before going inside for a surf and turf dinner, a bottle of French wine that Chandler ordered by name, and the artsy music of an Indonesian jazz singer. After dinner, they danced, and for the first time, Chelsea began to feel at ease in the arms of the man she loved.

With her eyes closed, her face nestled in his neck, his arms on her back, holding her closer than was necessary, or even appropriate, the rhythm of his all too familiar heartbeat helped her relax and she realized she was home, again. The only home she had ever really known or wanted.

She had Chandler back. It didn't matter what name he went by. It didn't matter that his nose was longer, or his jawbone was wider. This was Chandler, the man that she loved. The only man she would ever love. She was in his arms, again. Finally. Everything in the world suddenly seemed right.

"Do you remember the first time we danced?" she whispered in his ear.

"I do." he kissed her neck, soft, loving pecks, as she spoke. "Cammie's wedding. You were furious with me."

"I wasn't furious. Well, maybe I was, but only because I was so disappointed." She relaxed into his arms as the memories washed over her. "I thought Shiloh was the most incredible man I had ever met. A homeless drummer with the heart and soul of a poet."

"You were furious with me for not being homeless."

"No… maybe. I was furious because I didn't know you.

Or I thought I didn't know you…. I had shared so much of my soul with this deep, sensitive, beautiful man. And it turned out he was a spoiled rotten, overly indulged rich kid with a heroin problem and a string of women a mile long. At least that's what I thought that day. It took me a while to realize you were one and the same."

"Things aren't always as they seem, Chelsea."

"I know. You may me realize that regardless of your name, or your background, or your financial status, you were the wonderful man I had believed you to be." He drew back from their dancing embrace to look into her eyes.

"It's not a lot different from then to now, is it? You know, this drives me completely insane. You're like a chameleon. I fall madly in love with who you are, and then you morph into someone else."

"I don't change, Chelsea. Your perception of me, of who I am, changes, somewhat, but I'm the same person you met on the boulevard. I'm the guy who has loved you since the first moment I laid eyes on you. My financial status was different than you imagined it to be. Now my face is different. But inside I'm the same. I promise you; I haven't changed at all."

"Chandler…"

"It's true. There's not another woman in the world that I would say, stay with me, sleep in my arms, let me hold you, and I'll wait for however long it takes to make love to you…. I wouldn't waste my time on that. You know me better than that. But I'll do whatever I have to do, wait as long as I have to wait… no matter how frustrating, just to have you in my life. Damn woman, I love you. You have no idea how much I love you. It actually amazes me that I can love someone this much."

"Well, maybe the wait is not going to be all that long." She suggested, pressing her body closer to his.

"You think not?" he asked.

"I think we need to go home."

"Home?"

"Your home?"

"I want it to be your home, too."

"My home is with you. Wherever you are. That's my home."

"I think it's time we go home." His lips gently touched hers before he took her hand and led her off the dance floor.

"Set a speed record." She whispered as his boat pulled away from the dock just a few minutes later.

CHAPTER THIRTEEN

It was after midnight when they returned to the cabin cruiser. They walked in the door and were immediately in one another's arms.

All the hunger, the yearning, the intense need of three long years apart, consumed both of them as they quickly removed one another's clothing. She pulled him down onto the floor in front of the doorway, as the passion, so long denied, swept over both of them. Later when they were temporarily sated, he helped her up and they made their way toward the bedroom. The ridges of the cold hard ceramic tile had made creases on the skin of her back. He began to kiss the marks, as if to make them magically go away.

They made it as far as the sofa in the middle of the cabin where they made love again. This time with her on top, kissing his face, his neck, his shoulders, almost in a frenzy. They could not get enough of one another as their bodies melted together in the age-old rhythm. It was almost dawn before they finally made their way to the bed, and once again made love. Tired but so driven by their need for one another that even their exhaustion could not alleviate their passion.

Finally, totally fulfilled, reluctant to pull away but unable to continue, Chandler fell back against the soft silky sheets.

"I've missed you so much." He breathed. "I don't think I even realized how much I missed you until right now."

"I know." Chelsea sighed, contentedly. "I forgot how good we are together... that's probably a good thing. If I had remembered... I don't think I could have taken this separation."

"I love you so much. I can't believe how much I love you." He marveled at the depth of his own emotion.

"You keep saying that."

"It keeps being true." He exclaimed, pulling her close to him for another kiss... and it was then, that she saw it.

"Chan...uhm, Jean-Luc." She whispered. Her body suddenly stiff with fear.

"What's wrong, baby?"

"Shhh." She continued to whisper. "Don't react but there's someone standing on the deck, someone standing at the window. Someone is watching us."

In one swift move, Chandler turned over in the bed, quickly removed a revolver from a drawer in the nightstand table and charged toward the glass doors that opened out to the deck. The voyeur reacted immediately, turning, and running around the edge of the boat with Chandler following close behind.

Chelsea sat up on the bed, shaking as she wrapped the bed sheet around her naked body. Should she go after him? Was it safe to stay here alone? Should she call the police? She contemplated her options, becoming more frightened with each passing moment and then, suddenly the shadow of a man's silhouette appeared, once again, in the glass doorway, causing her to scream.

"It's ok. Calm down. It's ok." Chandler reassured her as

he pulled her back into his arms, still holding the gun in his hand.

"Who was that? Did you catch him?" she asked.

"No, I wasn't exactly dressed to go running down the dock after him." And, it was then, for the first time, she realized he had gone out after the voyeur, totally naked, himself. She chuckled at the thought of him running down the dock completely nude, but the concerned expression did not leave his face.

"Who was that? What did they want?"

"Probably just a pervert. It's ok Chelsea. You're safe. Don't be afraid."

"Do you have a lot of trouble with Peeping Toms here in the marina?" Chelsea asked.

"No. not that I know of." he admitted as he carefully put the gun back in the drawer of the nightstand. "I've never seen anyone outside. Of course, I didn't see…uhm, him. You did." Chandler confessed.

"So why do you have that gun?"

"Chandler Blake has a lot of enemies. So does Jean-Luc. The gun is necessary."

"You didn't have a gun when you were just Chandler Blake." She countered.

"Actually, baby, I did. I just never had any reason to let you see it."

"I don't like guns. They scare me." She declared, resolutely.

"I don't like them, either. They are scary. But not as scary as some of the things that could happen if I didn't have one to protect you… and myself."

"Do you really think the person watching was just a voyeur… or could t be someone who is after you? I want to know the truth. No matter how disturbing it might be. I want to know. Chandler, you don't think I've led the ISB to you, do you?" Chelsea was suddenly fearful.

"No. Not at all. If they still have you under surveillance, then, they know you came to Istanbul over a month ago and we've had no contact, whatsoever. They saw us meet last night, and you come home with me. Jean-Luc is well-known for picking up women in bars. He's done that for years. Long before I took on his persona. So, no. I don't think they would put it all together."

"So, then, who was it? The criminals that helped you establish this identity, maybe?"

"No, I don't think so. I did what they asked me to do. Made sure they got all their money back. They thanked me and wished me luck when we finished."

"So who then?" she demanded to know, unwilling to be placated.

"I don't know." He kissed her indulgently on her nose. "You know Chelsea, there's not a nefarious conspiracy behind everything that happens. Sometimes people just peep into windows because they are creeps."

"And you really believe that's what this is?" she asked, skeptically.

"I don't know what else it could have been." He reasoned as he slid back under the sheets and lay back on his pillow, pulling her down alongside him. She kissed his chest several times.

"Do you think we will ever have a nice, normal life?" she groaned.

"I hope not. Sounds boring as hell."

"Life with you will never be boring." Chelsea murmured, cuddling safely in Chandler's arms, and with all fear gone, she was suddenly very sleepy.

"Nor with you, baby." He kissed her forehead and then

gently stroked her hair until she had fallen into a deep sleep. He did not sleep, though. Not for a long time. Instead, he stared at the window, thinking who the voyeur might be.

He had been mostly honest with Chelsea. He was certain this was not the ISB… the execution was too sloppy; nor, did he think it was the European syndicate he had dealt with; they didn't care what he did or whom he did it with as long as they had their money.

But he also did not think it was random. Someone was definitely spying on them…. And what he had not told Chelsea was that he had caught a brief glimpse of the face as the voyeur ran away. It was a face he was sure he recognized. A face that could mean nothing but trouble.

He pulled Chelsea as close as was possible. Kissed her nose, her forehead, her cheek, several times, her lips curving into a slight smile as she slept; then, he closed his own eyes and tried to ignore the growing worry that their happily ever after might not be as easy as he had hoped.

CHAPTER FOURTEEN

Six weeks passed. Chelsea and Chandler settled into their new life together without further incident. There was no sign of the peeper. Chelsea seemed to have forgotten the entire thing and Chandler did nothing to remind her. He remained cautious, on the watch, though; going so far as to add surveillance equipment on the deck; a task he completed while Chelsea was at school; a task he neglected to mention when she came home.

With the passage of time, he began to relax. Maybe the peeper situation was not as dire as he first feared. It seemed as if things were working out better than he would have dared to hope. They became known, and accepted, as a couple, by both the people she worked with, and local people who had known the original Jean-Luc. They had an active social life, dining out with his friends several nights a week. They frequently attended live theater, art shows, concerts.

This was very unlike Chandler, who explained in private, that Jean-Luc had been a huge patron of the arts and thrived on the buzz of social activity that accompanied that patronage.

"It was one of the hardest things I had to deal with, when I became Jean-Luc. I tried to emulate his lifestyle as much as possible. Do things he did. But there were times I almost lost it. One week there were five charity fund-raisers, all of which he had always attended before. He, I, was expected to be there, at all of them… in a tux… smiling at strangers. Some of which weren't strangers… well, not to Jean-Luc. It was an insane amount of socializing. And, of course, the more I am around Jean-Luc's friends, the more likely I am to slip up and say the wrong thing. Somehow tip them off that I'm not who I claim to be. So that was worrisome as well. It was a long week. One of the longest of my life."

"Have you ever made a major mistake? Felt like you had tipped your hand?" Chelsea wanted to know.

"Nothing that I haven't been able to explain away. There have been a few slip ups, here and there. When it happens, when I say something that is totally antithetical to what Jean-Luc would be expected to say… I blame that on some aphasia from the brain injury…. So far, everyone seems to have accepted that explanation, but I still have to be careful. I've studied everything I could find on his life, but I don't know everything. I can't avoid an occasional slip-up, so I think the more I behave like him, the less likely anyone is to get suspicious."

Of course, as they soon learned, Chelsea was totally unlike anything Jean-Luc, a modern-day Lothario, had done before. He had been thirty-four years old when he passed, always had a woman with him, or, at the races, nearby, and yet there was no evidence any of these relationships had lasted more than two to three weeks.

"He changed after the wreck." Ajax explained to Charlotte who, in turn, brought the information to the school where it eventually filtered down to Chelsea.

"He became quieter, more introverted." Prior to the wreck, no one expected him to ever settle down with one woman, but in the months since he walked out of the hospital, he had become a vastly different man. Ajax was not at all surprised by the burgeoning relationship.

"Jean-Luc before the wreck, and Chelsea would not have made it through a weekend. Jean-Luc, as he is now… I am not surprised by this at all. He almost died… that has to change a man. Makes him re-evaluate his priorities. Makes him see what is really important." He theorized, and that theory caused most of the others, people who knew Jean-Luc only by reputation, to accept the one-hundred-and-eighty-degree personality pivot. Yes, most agreed. The wreck, the near-death experience was undoubtedly the explanation for his personality evolution, but it still did not stop people from being overly, and overtly, curious about the girl who had finally settled him down. The inquisitive looks, the sometimes-rude questions, were often difficult for Chelsea.

"So, you are Jean-Luc's new girl?" a museum curator, female, asked Chelsea, smirking as she spoke. It was a fund-raising tea at the Chora Museum. She made the mistake of wandering away from Chandler, Jean-Luc, as he spoke to a group of donors. She stood gazing fondly at a vivid fresco when the woman, tall, thin, dark eyes, and hair, dressed all in black, approached and hit her with a barrage of questions.

"You know Jean-Luc?" Chelsea questioned, already knowing the answer. It seemed everywhere they went, she ran in to a woman, multiple women, who had known Jean-Luc. Known in the biblical sense of knowing him intimately

"Yes, but of course. We have many good memories together." Her smile seemed warm and friendly… not always the case with Jean-Luc's former lovers.

"I knew him well before the accident… not well at all, now. He's quite different, now."

"Why do you say that?" Chelsea asked. As a dutiful girlfriend she was always looking for information that would help Chandler in his ruse.

"You. People who knew Jean-Luc before and meet you know, immediately, he is not the same man. He has changed dramatically."

"Because of me?"

"No, I don't think so. Not because of you. But you show us all that he has changed. You are American girl. He did not like American girls. Said they were boring in bed. Said he gave them such pleasure that he could never get rid of them, afterwards, even though he had no interest in repeating. He makes many jokes about skinny American model who laid down on bed, spread her legs and said, let me know when you have finished. He transformed her world, but it was bad mistake. He could not get rid of her. He was required to get court order forcing her to keep her distance. Too much trouble, he said. American girls are just too much trouble, for little pleasure. Obviously, you have taught him otherwise. He has, I'm sure, told you about this particular experience." The smirk was still on her face.

Chelsea gave what she hoped was her most enigmatic smile. A smile she had practiced in the mirror for this particular comment which she had heard several times before. Chandler had, in fact, told her the story of Jean-Luc, the American model, and the restraining order. The unfortunate situation had been well-covered in the tabloids and she knew the story was true. But she had decided that it was best to never confirm, or deny, anything. It was better, she decided, to be mysterious and aloof, than to risk saying something that might cause suspicion about his identity. There was enough reason to be suspicious, already.

Jean-Luc preferred women with olive skin, dark hair and eyes. Italian, Greek, and Egyptian women seemed to be his favorites. Chelsea's blonde hair and blue eyes had also caused a few raised eyebrows. Memory problems could be explained. As could a change in lifestyle. A complete change of taste was a little less understandable. People accepted it, but Chelsea worried, constantly, that she would be the one who did something, said something, that caused the whole house of cards to collapse.

"You worry too much." Chandler chided her on more than one occasion. "People believe I'm Jean-Luc. What choice do they have? Think about it. What's easier to believe? A stranger had plastic-surgery and stepped into Jean-Luc's life, or a horrible accident took its toll on an over-the-top personality?" If anyone ever even thought of the first possibility, they wisely did not articulate it. Chandler was accepted as Jean Luc. Chelsea was accepted as the object of his first serious affection. And their life together in Istanbul worked. Better than either would have expected. But there was, always, the still, small, anxiety-enticing voice in the back of her head, warning her that it could all blow-up at any moment.

Otherwise, she was blissfully happy. For the first time in their relationship, they had become exactly what she dreamed they could be. Their lives were perfect. She loved her job. She loved her life. Chandler seemed to be at peace, as well. As Jean-Luc, he had befriended a number of other boat dwellers in the marina where they lived. They visited back and forth, had cook-outs, drank beer, watched sporting events together. She laughingly compared it to life in suburbia...

albeit a floating suburbia, an international suburbia with neighbors from Italy, Great Britain, India, Egypt, and Algeria.

The peeper had not been explained to Chelsea's full satisfaction but, Olivia and Tony Leicester, a British couple who owned one of the larger boats in the marina, shared a similar experience with a peeper that had occurred several years earlier… also never explained.

"We were shagging on the sofa." Olivia told her as they sat beside a dockside fire pit, drinking beer, one night. "I looked up and there the pervert was. Just standing in front of the window, in plain view, dogging us. I screamed and gave him the finger. Tony took off after him… he was running down the side of the dock, pulling his pants up over his knees, and he tripped and put himself out of commission for more than a week. Never did find out who it was, but now that I know it's happened to you too… seems like we have a pervert in our mist. Afterwards, Tony and I just started making sure we have the blinds down when we are docked and shagging. If you wanna shag with the sea as a backdrop, you just need to take the boat out. Only real way to guarantee privacy, anymore. I don't care how perverted the prat is, I doubt if he's going to swim a hundred kilometers or more to see someone else get off."

"See." Chandler reassured her later that night when she shared the Leicester's story… "They are as normal as they can be." Tony was a journalist with the London Times on a long-time foreign assignment, Olivia, a well-respected influencer, who blogged about foreign cuisine. "There are just peepers in the world. Our background just made us a little more paranoid about the whole thing, but I'm sure that's all it was." Chelsea nodded in agreement. She had put the matter behind her, not given it much thought in several weeks;

nevertheless, she was relieved when she learned that someone else had experienced the same situation.

"Has it crossed your mind that we are actually happy?" she mused one cool Saturday afternoon as they stood in line to ride a roller coaster. They had been together for over two months; it was fall break at the American School; and she and Chandler had taken the train through Romania, Hungary, Austria and Bulgaria into Freiburg, Germany, where Oktoberfest was being celebrated. They had drunk German beer and ate traditional barbarian food; sat by an open fire as an old man shared tales of the German goblins that lived in the Black Forest. The storyteller spoke in German only. Chelsea didn't understand a word. But, between Chandler's whispered translations, and the storyteller's animated behavior, she was sufficiently terrified. Totally into the celebration, she had actually dressed in a dirndl one day, for the street dance, but Chandler refused to put on the Lederhosen.

"Chelsea, baby… I love you with all my heart. I love you so much I would die for you. Actually, now that I think of it… I kind of did die for you." He joked. "But no way in hell am I going out in public wearing tight leather ass shorts."

"Party pooper." She teased him before they left the hotel, but as they walked through the streets, she quickly realized that most of the other male tourists obviously felt the same way. Men in jeans and women in aprons were everywhere to be seen.

After the roller coaster ride, they walked down to the Ferris Wheel, the top of which provided a view beyond the town, to the woodland known as The Black Forest, which was beginning to show the brilliant colors of autumn. After several complete revolutions, they stopped at the top. Chandler had pulled her close to him for a kiss when Chelsea's innate sense of apprehension kicked in. She shivered suddenly. Not surprising since the sun had just gone down on what had been a cooler than normal afternoon. But there was more to it than that.

"Want my jacket?" Chandler offered.

"No. I'm not cold." She stammered.

"You're shaking like a leaf." He chided her, as he removed his coat.

"Not because of the cold though. I think someone is watching us…"

"What? Where?" He looked around and saw no sign of any surveillance.

"I don't know. I just can feel it?"

"You feel like someone is watching us?"

"Don't make light of this." She snapped. "I developed a sixth sense about this when I was in Mississippi and the ISB was on my tail everywhere I went. I know when I'm being watched. It is a finely honed instinct and I'm telling you someone is watching us."

"OK." Chandler nodded, a confused expression on his face. "Maybe someone is just checking out who is stopped at the top." He suggested.

"No. It's more than that. Stop arguing with me about this. I know what I'm talking about. Someone is watching us. Intentionally."

"OK. I'll take your word for it." Chandler conceded, not really convinced, himself, but quickly realizing that arguing the point with Chelsea would be futile. He looked around the vicinity, once again, as the Ferris wheel rotated toward the ground; saw no sign of anyone paying them even a modicum of interest. Still, there was something about Chelsea's determination that made him take her concerns seriously. Someone was watching them. But who? And where were they?

Chelsea was visibly uncomfortable for the rest of the

evening. Constantly looking over her shoulder for any sign of… who… she did not know. After a traditional meal of Schweinebraten and knodel, supplied by a street vendor, they returned to their hotel room, drank a delicious hot chocolate and peppermint schnapps toddy, made love, and slept, peacefully, arms and legs entwined.

The next morning, she did not think of the incident. Chandler was happy to see that she was carefree, back to the happy woman he loved… but her emotions came back full force that afternoon when the text notification signal sounded on her phone. Chelsea took the phone from the pocket on her denim jacket and studied the message carefully for a moment as her face fell.

"What's wrong, baby. What's wrong?"

"Remember yesterday when I told you we were being watched."

"Yeah."

"I was right. We've made Online Snoop Magazine's Front Cover today… kissing at the top of the Ferris wheel. Listen to this…]*Jean-Luc Moreau Steps Out* is the headline. It says that you've been in a self-imposed isolation since the wreck, but you were obviously enjoying your Oktoberfest Holiday with your latest girl of the moment. Chelsea Simmons, an American girl who readers may remember was romantically linked with the troubled son of Senator Isaiah Blake before his suicide three years ago. Geez… makes me sound like a dang celebrity hopper." Chelsea lamented.

"I'm sorry, baby."

"That's not the worst part of it. Guess who sent me this link."

"I don't know. Your mom?" he guessed.

Chelsea shook her head negatively. "I wish. This is even worse. It's from Cammie."

"Cammie?"

"Your sister. Chandler's sister. Remember her?" There was an edge to her voice Chandler had rarely heard.

"Of course, I remember her. Did she just send that? Any message?"

"Yeah, this is what she says… "Chelsea, saw this on Facebook this morning. I won't lie, it hurt, but, only for a minute. We all love you. We know how much you loved Chandler and how much he loved you. And we want you to have a happy life. You look happy here. Happier than I ever expected to see you look, again. And I'm really glad for you. Mom and Dad will be too… eventually. You know how they are. Love you. Stay in touch."

"Oh, man. She's as good as my Mom with that passive aggressive shit, isn't she?" Chandler shifted uncomfortably in his seat.

"She's not being passive aggressive."

"Sounds to me like she's trying to make you feel guilty."

"She's not. She loves you Chandler. So do your parents… and don't roll your eyes at me. I know they are deeply flawed, but they loved you. I was at your funeral. I saw their agony. And it hasn't lessened. Three years and the pain is just as intense, just as raw, as it was the day we buried you. They have not healed. Not even a little bit. I saw them not long before you sent Jason to recruit me. They were opening a foundation to combat sex trafficking in memory of you and Cissy. They are still heartbroken. Cammie, your mother, your father. All three of them. They have never gotten over your death and they never will."

"It couldn't be avoided. You know that."

"Yeah, I know. That's the only reason I went along with it. But Chandler you promised me you'd let them know you were alive as soon as you could."

"We are just now getting settled into our lives together."

"We *are* settled into our lives together. No one suspects who you really are. You've assured me of that a hundred times, at least. We've made it to the other side of this nightmare. It's time to tell them the truth. Honestly, I'm surprised they don't already know. At the ceremony dedicating the foundation your Uncle Doug wanted to tell them…"

"You told him not to, didn't you?"

"He was thinking it had been so long since we heard from you that you were probably dead. I was beginning to think so, as well, but I asked him to hold off for six more months. I wasn't ready to give up on you. But you're fine. We're together. We're happy. They deserve some happiness as well. Doug is going to tell them, eventually… but I'm sure they would rather hear it from you."

"You're right. I know you're right. But I don't know how to work the logistics. I'm comfortable being Jean-Luc, and I don't believe anyone has a clue… but if I go hopping across the pond to visit with them, on top of the fact that you and I are together, someone might get suspicious. This is going to be hard to work."

"No it isn't. Cammie sent me the email. I've stayed in contact with your family. It would make sense that I would want your parents to meet my new love. I'll invite them over."

"You actually think they'll travel eight thousand miles to meet the man you are replacing me with?"

"Yeah, I think they might. Cammie will do it. And I think your mom would go for it as well. She's been seeing psychics… trying to contact you."

"What?"

"Yeah, I know, it's bad, but evidently, they told her they have to be nice to me… you won't speak to them from beyond unless they are… so, I think she'd be afraid to say no. And if she agrees your dad will come along. Plus, Doug is probably going to figure it all out when I invite them over to meet you, so if they try to get out of it, he will convince them."

Chandler sighed.

"You know I'm right about this Chandler. They deserve to know. When you first came up with this plan, you told me you would let them know in just a few months…"

"I didn't know ISB was going to be tailing you for over a year and I didn't know I was going to have to assume a new identity."

"I know, baby. I understand what happened. Things didn't go according to plan. But we are good now. We are together. We are out in public. Cammie saw this picture and it didn't cross her mind this might be you. We are free and clear… they deserve to know the truth." Chelsea picked up her telephone.

"What are you doing?"

"I'm calling Cammie. I'm going to ask her to come to Istanbul for a visit…tell her I want her to meet my new love."

"That's cold."

"I know… and I'm sure she'll think I'm being quite heartless. But she'll forgive me when she meets you."

CHAPTER FIFTEEN

Cammie was reading *The Velveteen Rabbit* to her eighteen-month-old daughter, Chandler, when the phone rang. Chelsea. She sighed as she carefully sat the baby into her playpen... "OK sweetie, let mommy talk to Aunt Chelsea." she said. She took a deep breath before answering. This was going to be hard, but she needed to be strong. As much as she ached over the loss of her brother, she knew Chelsea's pain was a hundred times worse. Be supportive, she told herself. Do it for Chandler.

"Chelsea." She answered brightly. Too brightly. It sounded phony, insincere.

"Hi, Cams." Chelsea paused, for a moment. "I got your text."

"Yeah... I knew we hadn't heard from you much for the last few weeks and when I saw that picture, I thought, well, maybe you felt strange about it... because of, well, you know. So, I just wanted to let you know, I know about it. I'm going to break it to Mom and Dad in the next couple of days... It's cool with me. And it'll be good with them, too. We love you. We want you to be happy." Cammie was glad she was having this conversation on the phone rather than in person. There would have been no way she could have hidden the tears that had come into her eyes.

"Thank you. Actually, that's why I'm calling. I've been meaning to call you for a couple of weeks. I want you to meet Jean-Luc. I want you and your parents to meet him. Is there any way you could all come to Istanbul?"

"You want us to come to Istanbul?"

"Yeah. I really need for you to do this… for me. I need your support. It's hard, you know. He's a good guy, but I still think about Chandler every day and well, I need your approval."

"Well… ok." Cammie grimaced as she wondered how in the world she was going to be able to stand this. "I guess I could ask Mac to take some time off. We could come. I'm not sure about Mom and Dad. Chelsea, they love you and they want you to be happy, but this is going to be hard for them…. You're asking a lot here. Surely you know that."

"I know. And I'm sorry, but I need for them to do it for me, anyway. I've never asked Chandler's family for anything before. You know that. You guys have been great but that's been your choice. I haven't asked you to do anything. I'm asking now. I need you to come and give your approval. Tell them, Cammie. Tell them I need this. It will mean everything. I really want you and them to come and meet Jean-Luc. I need you to do this. It's important to me. Like the most important thing in the world. Please. Tell them I need all of you to come to Istanbul."

"I'll do the best that I can." Cammie promised. After hanging up the phone she gently picked up a picture that had been made at her wedding. Chandler, with a glass of champagne in his hand, smiling. Standing beside her. Giving her brotherly love and support on the biggest day of her life. He was so beautiful, so handsome, and he looked happy. Later on, she had learned that Chelsea had also been at the wedding. She was a plus one with another guest.

"We had met before." Chandler explained to his sister. "I liked her a lot, but my life was such a mess, I thought it was better to just not pull her into it. That day, I thought, well, I'm going to have to at least give this a chance. See where it goes. And it changed my life. Cammie, that girl changed my life."

The tears were flowing furiously now. His life had been a train wreck, but somehow, it seemed to turn around. Chelsea turned it around. And for the first time, in years, she and her family had hope that he would get it all together. It was not to be. But, for slightly over a year, he had been happy, Chelsea had made him happy, and knowing that he had that one happy year meant everything now. Of course, she would go to Istanbul to meet Jean-Luc. So would her parents. She would insist upon it. This was for the girl who was able to look beyond all the flaws and see her brother for the wonderful man that he was. They owed her this much.

CHAPTER SIXTEEN

It took some coaxing, but Cammie prevailed on her parents. Chandler's uncle Doug was also insistent. Senator Isaiah Blake, Chandler's father, had been outraged that Chelsea had even made such a request, and Veronica, his mother, simply refused to go.

"I'm sorry. I wish her all the best." She said. "But no. Absolutely not. I can't watch her move on with her life with another man while my son is cold and alone, turning into dust in the ground." She declared, stubbornly.

"Mom, Dad, you're going. I'm not going to take no for an answer. We have to do this."

"I don't have to do anything." Veronica had snapped back. "And I'm not going to go and meet that man. No, that's just asking too much. It's too much."

"Ronnie. Chandler loved that girl. And he would expect us to love her too. The fact that she wants us all to meet him should tell you how much she loved him, how much she wants to keep his memory alive. And we are going to do it. We are going to go and meet the man. We are going to do it for Chandler." Doug knew, of course, that Chandler had not died the night that the body was found in his house, a gunshot wound to the face. He wasn't at all sure what Jean-Luc Moreau had to do with Chandler. Plastic surgery, an assumed identity, did not cross his mind. But he felt certain that this was all a set-up to reveal that Chandler was still alive, and he was determined his younger sister, Chandler's mother, would be there for what would certainly prove to be a startling revelation.

CHAPTER SEVENTEEN

It was the week before the American Thanksgiving when they arrived in Istanbul. They had chosen the date, but it occurred to Chelsea, that it was a perfect choice. After the visit, they would have many reasons to be thankful.

Chandler was nervous, fidgety, even, behaving completely out of character. He was usually cool, calm, in control. But, not on this day. Chelsea watched him as he paced around the room. Her heart overflowing. This was the man she loved. He worked hard to project an image of aloofness. He put on quite a show of being detached from familial emotions. But they were there. He loved his mom, his dad, his sister. And, today, try as he may, he couldn't hide it. He was excited to see them, again. Anxious about their reaction, but oh so ready to be reunited.

"I am the one that should be nervous." Chelsea told him, a teasing tone to her voice, although, she knew that there was a large degree of truth in what she was about to say. "They are going to be so happy to know you are alive… they won't even think to be mad at you. Me, on the other hand… I can already hear your dad… he's going to say….” She put her hands on her hips, assumed a harsh face and in a gruff tone of voice, continued… “Chelsea, we were good to you, accepted you into our family, loved you… and you kept this from us. Let us suffer for three years…” She sighed. “I'm the one who is going to bear the brunt of their derision. I'm the one who should be nervous.”

“You're about half-right in that.” Chandler conceded. “They'll be madder at you than me, but Doug is going to be the one who really catches hell. Fortunately, he can handle it.” His Uncle Doug had been the stabilizing influence on their highly dysfunctional family for as long as Chandler could remember. He controlled the purse strings which put him at the pinnacle of power within their family.

Doug and Veronica Cameron had been born two years apart, to one of the first families of California. Doug was the elder of the two and always protective of his younger sister.

They had grown-up in a world of incredible wealth and privilege in Monterey County, California where they owned miles of ocean front property. The family had been a horse family for over a hundred years, raising some of the finest thoroughbreds in the United States.

One of Veronica's first memories was a Kentucky Derby where a Cameron family horse won the race. And, later, in their teen years, another of their horses, one that Veronica had assisted in training, had actually won two legs of the Triple Crown. From that point forward, it was her life's ambition to repeat that accomplishment, and better it with a Triple Crown winning horse.

While in college, back East, she met Isaiah Blake, a handsome, young man, without a penny to his name. He was poor, but brilliant. A scholarship student who worked at a local bar to pay his living expenses. It had been love at first sight for

Veronica. Used to girls throwing themselves at him, he had been less impressed but, he warmed up to the relationship considerably after he learned of her vast family wealth. Many warned her of his less than noble intentions, but she paid no attention. The romance was fast and furious. To the horror of her parents, who were among the many who thought he was not worthy of their daughter, they eloped at the end of her freshman year of college, just months after meeting.

Veronica's father had taken one look at young Isaiah, judged him to be a gold-digger who would certainly break his daughter's heart. "Nothing I can do to save her heart, now." He said. "But I sure can save her money." And with that one comment, he revised his will, leaving his vast holdings entirely to his son....

"I know you love your sister. I trust you to deal fairly with her. It's not my intention that she be penniless. She's been indulged her entire life. I want that to continue." He explained, in the letter that was read at the time the will was probated. "But I don't want that rapscallion absconding with money it's taken generations for my family to amass. Doug, make sure she has what she needs. Make sure she has what she wants. But everything is yours. Veronica gets nothing and neither does her good for nothing husband."

Doug honored his father's wishes to the letter. So much so, that three wives found his incessant coddling of his younger sister unacceptable. After the third divorce, Doug had determined to never marry, again. Instead, he enjoyed the company of a number of women while dedicating his life to his sister and her children.

Veronica, and by extension, Isaiah and their children, had lived their lives as wealthy individuals. Doug made sure of that. No whim went unrealized. Isaiah used Cameron money to run for Congress and later on for the US Senate. He had become an enormously successful US Senator. The Blakes lived a glamorous Washington lifestyle… but the bill was footed by Doug.

At age nineteen, when Chandler was first recruited for a special undercover college assignment, by the FBI, he had been strongly admonished against sharing his new career with his whole family… but he was required to give the information to one person who could be notified in case of an emergency. He chose his uncle. Doug had always known about Chandler's occupation, and when Chandler decided to take drastic steps to remove himself from the ISB, he knew about that as well. He was among the party that came to Turkey, ostensibly, to meet Chelsea's new lover. And while Chandler did not intend to expose Doug's knowledge of his double life, he felt sure it would come to light. And he was equally sure there would be hell to pay for keeping the horrible secret.

CHAPTER EIGHTEEN

Rather than being on public display in the marina in Istanbul, they met in Amasra, Turkey, a small resort town on the Black Sea. Jean-Luc owned a charming stone-walled cottage nestled there on a wooded cliff that overlooked the water. From what Chandler had been able to piece together, this was a place where he had frequently met with the mysterious Andrea, who he and Chelsea had deduced was obviously a married woman. It was private, secluded and would not be a place that the paparazzi could easily photograph visitors. That would be important to a man courting a married woman. It was equally important for the Blake family reunion.

The cottage was warm, cozy, homey. Three of the four walls in the living area were lined with bookshelves that contained great works of literature. A stereo system wired through the walls, featured playlists that included symphonies by the masters. Fine china, Frijsenborg, by Royal Copenhagen, was displayed in an antique cabinet in the dining room and the floral design seemed to match the flowers that were growing in the small garden that bordered the tile patio outside. This was not the home of the high-rolling, race car driver that Jean-Luc had shown the world. This was the home of an intellectual. This was the home of a couple in love. This was the home Chelsea had dreamed of sharing with Chandler.

"I think I could live here the rest of my life..." She said, an hour after they had arrived. She was standing by the window, staring as the sapphire-colored ocean, a thousand feet below, crashed on the breakers.

"You wouldn't get bored?" Chandler teased, sliding his arms around her waist, pulling her close to him, as he nuzzled her neck.

"With you? Never." She insisted. She turned to give him a kiss and caught a glimpse of the long black Mercedes limo snaking its way down the drive to the front door. She nodded toward the window, and he turned, a look of trepidation covering his face. This had to be done. It was past due, and they both knew it. But there was no predicting how his parents were going to react.

"Showtime." He whispered, brushing his lips against hers, before he turned to walk into the study. They had decided it would be best if she greeted them at the door, got them inside, and settled, before he made an appearance.

"We've got this." He promised, with more confidence than he felt, as he shut the door behind him, while Chelsea walked toward the front door, inhaling deeply several times. She opened the door and smiled as Doug, Ronnie, the Senator, Cameron, and her husband Mac walked toward her.

Doug reached her first, kissed her lightly on the cheek. "You look beautiful, Chelsea. Beautiful and happy." He beamed, a warm smile on his face, a knowing expression in his eyes.

"Come on in..." Her voice was weak and fraught with emotion.

"This is a lovely cottage." Cameron was impressed. "Did you do the decorating?"

"No. It was decorated before… before I met Jean-Luc."

"It looks like you." Ronnie said, a tinge of melancholy in her voice. "This is just the kind of place I pictured you and… well, it's really lovely." She sighed, dramatically

"It's beautiful, but I don't understand why we are here. Why didn't we just meet in Istanbul. We've been driving forever…. What is this? You just want to show us how well things are going for you?" Isaiah complained.

"Isaiah…" Ronnie narrowed her eyes and spoke sharply.

"Sorry. I'm doing the best I can but, well, never mind. I'm doing the best I can. That's all I can tell you." He muttered contritely but there was still an edge to his voice.

"No, I'm the one who should be sorry." Chelsea smiled. "Sorry for the inconvenience. I know it's a long drive, but we thought it was better if this happened here. It's more secluded. We wanted this meeting to be private. Out of the public eye. That was extremely important. You'll understand why soon enough. Just have a seat. Doug… the bar is over in the corner… you might want to make everyone a drink. A stiff one." She smiled and he nodded, walking across to the bar.

"So, where is this Mr. Wonderful you wanted us to meet?" Isaiah asked, resentfully.

"Isaiah…" Ronnie cautioned him again.

"No, I need to say this… and, Chelsea, just so you understand, this is coming only from me. My family cares about you. I do, too. We all care. And we are glad you've been able to move on with your life…. That's what Chandler would have wanted. He wouldn't have wanted you to grieve over him, forever. He would have wanted you to move on. And we support you in doing just that. We really do. I promise. We are happy for you. But knowing you've replaced Chandler in your heart is hard enough on all of us. Flying ten hours, spending a night in a hotel, and then getting up at the crack of dawn to drive six more hours…. That might be asking a little bit too much. Frankly, I'm surprised that you would be so lackadaisical about our feelings. I, for one, would like an explanation. Do you really just not understand how difficult this is?"

"Yes sir. I do understand. But, well, I really can't explain… I think once you meet Jean-Luc, it will make more sense. I think he can make you understand better than I can." She walked to the door of the downstairs study and opened it. "They're here."

Chandler took a final gulp from the glass of Scotch in his hand, placed it on the fireplace mantle and walked through the door into the living room where he came face to face with his family.

It had been three long years, and, to his surprise, the moment was far more emotional than he had imagined it would be. He fought against tears as he looked from one face to the next. His heart breaking at the sight. They were miserable. He could see it in their eyes. There was an emptiness, a vacancy that was unrecognizable. Had he done this to them? Had his faked death really caused them this kind of pain?

He felt an enormous weight of guilt and at the same time, an incredible sense of gratitude. They believed he was dead. They knew how he loved Chelsea, and so, putting their own feelings aside, they were there to support the woman he loved, the woman they believed was moving on with her life. They were there, but it was taking its toll. Especially on his dad.

He had not had a good relationship with his parents in years. But he loved them. And he knew they loved him.

Seeing this misery, knowing that he was responsible, hurt him. It literally caused physical pain.

"Well, this is, uhm, Jean-Luc." Chelsea stammered, the emotion of the moment hitting her hard.

Isaiah, with no recognition in his eyes, stood up and offered a handshake. "Good to meet you, sir. You're involved with a fine young woman. Chelsea is a one of a kind. I want you to know, we consider her part of our family. She says you're a good guy, and you need to be. She was deeply loved by our son. She deserves that kind of devotion from you as well. You better be good to her. Or you will answer to me."

"Yes sir." Chandler nodded, his eyes softening in gratitude to the father that did not recognize him.

"Oh Cammie…" Chelsea said, responding to her friend. Cammie was sitting on the sofa, with tears running down her face.

"I'm sorry, Chelsea." She sniffled, furiously wiping away the tears. "Jean-Luc, I apologize. What my dad said is true. Chelsea is part of our family and if she loves you, then we love you, too. This is just harder than I expected it to be…. I'm sorry." She choked on the words as she laid her head on her husband's shoulder and began to quietly sob.

Veronica stood from her seat and walked to Chandler. She stood looking at him, face to face. Her eyes narrow and pensive. She put her slender hands-on Chandler's shoulders, caressed his face gently with her fingers before turning to Chelsea. "What the hell is going on here?" she literally screamed the words.

"Ronnie…." Doug walked toward her, offering her a glass of Scotch.

"I don't want a damned drink. I want an explanation and it better be a good one. What the hell is going on?"

"I'm sorry Jean-Luc, my wife is…"

"Shut-up, Isaiah. I don't need you making apologies for me. I have a right to be angry. And I am. I'm freakin' furious. Look at him. Can you not see it? Are you blind? This isn't Jean-Luc… this is Chandler. Look at him. This is Chandler. Can't you see it? How the hell are you standing there? How the hell are you alive. I can't believe this. I can't believe it. His face is changed but, look at the eyes… look at him. This is Chandler. I don't understand. Someone explain this to me. Chelsea? What the hell is going on? You know who this is, don't you? You know this is Chandler. Tell them. Tell Isaiah, tell Cammie. It's Chandler. I'd know him anywhere. How the hell can you not see that? Cammie…. Look at him… don't you know who this is?"

"Ronnie, calm down, this is not…" Isaiah protested.

"Hell, yes, it is. This is my son. I know my son. I carried him in my body for nine long months. I endured twenty-one hours of hard labor giving birth to him. I know my son…" Ronnie turned back to Chandler, glared angrily at him, and then, without warning slapped him hard across the face. "Tell him. Tell your idiot father who you are. Tell him now."

It was the moment of truth. Not exactly the way he and Chelsea had envisioned it, but it was the moment of truth.

"She's right, Dad." Chandler confessed, just as Ronnie's hand slapped him, once again, across the other cheek, and this time, the band of her sapphire ring cut into his face causing blood to spurt out onto her hand.

"You damned asshole. I never beat you as a child, but right now, I'd like to take a strap to you and whack you for the next ten years. What the hell is wrong with you? You let me think you were dead? You let me think you committed suicide? How could you do that? How could you?" she turned to Chelsea. "And you, you little bitch….

"Mom…." Chandler interrupted.

"Don't mom me. This little bitch is going to explain herself. Chelsea, I want to know what we did to deserve this kind of treatment from you. We let you into our family. Welcomed you with open arms. We loved you. Even after we thought he was dead, we loved you. Even after we thought he killed himself because you left him, we continued to be kind to you. We worried about how you were doing. We prayed you'd be able to move on and have a life, even though we knew that was going to hurt us when it happened. We cared about you. And all the time… all the damned time, you knew he was alive. You let me think he was dead, and you knew he was alive? Didn't you? Admit it." She screeched accusingly as she moved toward Chelsea in an aggressive manner.

Chandler quickly stepped between his mother and the woman he loved. "OK mom. Chelsea hated every minute of this. She's not to blame. I am. It's totally on me. I did this. I'm the one you need to blame."

"I do blame you. I'm so mad at you, I swear, right at this minute I could kill you myself. But that doesn't excuse her. I blame both of you. I've been through hell and back in the past three years… and you're alive the whole time." Her voice had begun to tremble.

"You're alive while I'm hurting. You're alive while…. You're alive." She dissolved into tears as she wrapped her arms around his shoulders and pulled him close to her. "My baby is alive. My baby is alive." She sobbed, smacking him hard, this time on the back of the head, with her open palm.

Isaiah stood, almost in shock, looking from Chandler, to Veronica, to Chelsea as the conversation took place around him.

"Have you all lost your mind?" he finally asked. His voice slow and steady. His tumultuous emotions revealed only by the deep crimson color of his face. "Have you all taken leave of your senses? Ronnie what the hell is wrong with you? Look at this boy. This is not Chandler… And you, who the hell are you to call me dad? I'm not your dad. You don't have the right to call me that. My son is dead… he's the only one with the right to call me that. My wife has obviously lost her mind, and maybe you think you are being kind to indulge her insanity. But whatever you're thinking… don't call me dad. You don't have the right to do that."

"Dad…it's me…. Mom is right. It's me. I am your son. I am Chandler."

"No, you're not. This doesn't make any sense at all. You died…. I mean, Chandler died. He died. You're not him. He's dead."

"Dad, look, I can explain…"

"No, hell, no… don't call me dad. I told you, you don't have that right. You're not my son. I don't know what the hell is going on here, but I won't be part of this mass delusion. I buried my son. I buried him three years ago…" his voice broke as he spoke. "You're not my son. My son is dead."

Cammie had stopped crying. "Chelsea?" she asked as she pushed passed her mother, to come face to face with Chandler. Chelsea nodded. Cammie took his face in her hands, stared momentarily in his eyes before wrapping her arms around her brother's shoulders, pulling him close to her.

"I'm going to kill you." She said, her voice trembling. "I'm going to hug you for a while. And then, I'm going to show you pictures of your niece… she's nineteen months old and she knows she was named after her wonderful Uncle Chandler who went to be with the angels. She's beautiful. And I want you to see her. I want you to meet her. I've wanted her to meet you every day of her life. So, I want you to meet her… I want her to meet you… and then after all that happens… I'm going to kill you. I am. I'm going to make you wish you had died when you let us think you did. I'm going to kill you."

Chandler's arms slid down around his sister's waist. He pulled her close, picked her up off the ground. "I'm so sorry, Cammie." He whispered. "I'm so sorry I hurt you. I'm so sorry." His voice breaking as she began to, at first, whimper, and then sob loudly.

Isaiah watched his wife and his daughter. Ronnie was touching this stranger's face, his arm, his shoulder, with awe and wonder. It was as if she had found the Holy Grail. Cammie had her arms wrapped around the stranger and was sobbing. Mac, Cammie's husband, shrugged, at Isaiah's questioning look.

"What the hell is wrong with all of you?" he exploded.

"Why don't we just all sit down." Doug suggested as he put a drink in Isaiah's hand. "Why don't we just all sit down and let Chandler explain what's going on, and where he's been?"

"Chandler? Did you say Chandler?" Isaiah shouted, rubbing his hands across his face and through his hair in frustration. "Don't tell me you're giving into this nonsense. too? Am I the only sane person left in this room?"

"Dad, Doug is right… Have a seat. Everybody have a seat. I'll explain this all…"

"Don't call me Dad!" Isaiah thundered. "I swear boy, if you call me Dad again, I'll kill you, myself." Isaiah's voice was so loud, so strong, that the crystal lamp on the fireplace mantle shook.

"Fine, Senator Blake. Have a seat. Mom, Cammie, Doug, Mac… come on, sit down. It's a long story and I'm going to tell you everything."

CHAPTER NINETEEN

"I wanted out before I met Chelsea. I didn't like the life I was living. I didn't like the person I had become. I wanted out. And when I met her, when I realized this was someone I could have a real life with…" he picked up her hand, opened her five fingers and gently kissed her palm. "I had to get out…it was just not as easy as I had expected it to be."

For almost two hours the Blake family had sat, listening, as Chandler explained the whole story. A suspect in the Cissy Westbrooks disappearance, his family had never known that he had been the one who eventually, anonymously, discovered her true kidnappers. The FBI, impressed with his investigative skills, had recruited him for another job on another campus. And so it began.

He had enjoyed the FBI… should have stayed with it… but, he was a risk taker, a rule breaker. He had been admonished several times about the necessity of following legal protocol during investigations. He was a firm believer in doing whatever he had to do to get the evidence he needed. It was an ongoing bone of continuous contention between his superiors and himself.

They wanted him to follow the rules, he wanted to get the criminal, and he didn't care how he did it. He was good, extremely good, at his job. If not, he would have probably been terminated. Because his skills were better than most, they put up with him. But it was a constant battle… they were always trying to reign him in, while he pushed the limits more and more with every case he investigated.

And then, at age twenty-four, he was recruited by the ISB… the International Security Bureau, a top-secret international crime bureau. Deep State. Very few rules. It was, they explained, made to order for his particular skill set, for his determination, his dedication to mission.

He had been desperate for revenge at the time. Desperate to find the notorious King, an international criminal who ran a sex trafficking syndicate that was ultimately responsible for the disappearance of his college girlfriend. He was limited in the FBI. He had gotten to the point where he spent more time dodging FBI oversight than he spent chasing the criminals. ISB offered him a freer reign. He jumped at that offer.

"With the FBI, I fought against crimes that were taking place in the present. The ISB offered me the chance to go after the people who kidnapped Cissy and ruined my life when I was eighteen years old. I wanted to do that. I wanted to bring those people down. I wanted to get my revenge." It was only after he had made the switch that he realized he had made a deal with the devil. He had not understood, not given thought, to the idea that the FBI had an exit door. He could leave anytime he chose. The ISB was a different story.

"You're trying to tell us that you never did drugs?" Isaiah asked, his voice monotone from the shock of all that he had heard.

"Never is a big word..." Chandler chuckled. "I've smoked quite a bit of pot in my life. It's in the job description. Most criminals do, and if I were infiltrating a crime ring, then I would smoke pot with them. A few times it got a little more serious than that... I snorted cocaine when I had to. If I found myself in a situation where I had to choose between coke and possibly blowing my cover.... snorting the coke wasn't as dangerous as a cartel could be if they had ever gotten suspicious of me. Not by half."

"That's actually how I found out he was an agent." Chelsea had mostly listened as the conversation took place, but this was something she felt they needed to understand.

"Chandler turned up on my doorstep one night completely wasted. I was so upset because I had convinced myself that all those rumors about what a reckless guy he was were just wrong... and then, he stumbles into my apartment, falls on the floor and announces he got some bad coke. I was horrified. I couldn't believe it. He was mumbling on and on about drugs not usually affecting him this way and I said why would you do something this stupid? Why would you mess up your life with drugs? And, he said he had to maintain his cover.

The minute he said it, I knew. It all made sense. The man I knew him to be versus the man that everyone said he was. I knew he was a good guy. His press said he wasn't. I had been trying to figure it out and the minute he said those words, it just all fell into place." Chelsea laughed.

"But even then, he wouldn't admit it. The next day when he was not high, anymore, I told him what he said, and he totally denied it. He didn't admit it for a long time... But I knew... I knew, and he knew that I knew, and even then, he wouldn't admit it. He didn't admit it until." she bit her lip. This was Chandler's story to tell.

"He didn't admit it until what?" Veronica asked. "What happened? Why did the two of you do this to us?"

"I quit. I told my handler at the ISB I was finished. I said I'm done. I'm not doing this any longer. They harassed me for a couple of weeks, I didn't relent, so they grabbed Chelsea."

"What?" Isaiah asked. "What do you mean they grabbed her? Like kidnapping? Is that what you mean?"

"That is exactly what I mean. They kidnapped her. They only kept her for a few hours.... just long enough to make sure I knew she was gone, and they had her. They told me that I needed to do what I was told, because they could get her, anytime they wanted to get her. I knew then I had to do something more drastic."

"So, you faked your death and put us through three years of hell?" Isaiah exhaled forcefully as he rubbed his temples with each hand. "Chandler, son, let me just ask you this? You do know who I am? Right? I mean, throughout the years, you have not shown me a lot of respect... but I do hold an important, very respectable position in the United States government. You may not think much of me as a father, or a person, but I have a considerable amount of power. Do you understand that?"

"Yes sir, of course I do."

"Of course you do. Great. So, just out of curiosity, I have to know, did it ever cross your mind to come and tell me this story? Let me use that power, use my connections, to help get you out of this mess? I could have convened a committee to look into the ISB? I could have called the Pentagon. I could have called the damned President if I needed to do so."

Chandler shook his head negatively. "And that's why I couldn't tell you."

"What?" Isaiah asked. "What's wrong with that idea? You

wanna tell me that taking some help from your dad is worse than letting the whole damn world think you committed suicide?"

"Whose body was that, anyway?" Ronnie asked. "The body they found in your beach house?"

"A John Doe from the morgue. He had apparently died of a drug overdose so the tracks on his arms helped with the illusion." Chandler explained.

"And you just shot the poor guy's face off?" Isaiah asked.

"He didn't feel a thing." Chandler answered, ironically.

"Good grief, I have never heard such a story in my life. Doug, I need another drink." Isaiah continued. "And Chandler, I need an answer to my original question… you thought faking your death was preferable to letting me get you out of this mess?"

"No, not preferable. I just knew you couldn't get me out of it."

"The hell you say… I would have gone to the President on this one… he would have…"

"Dad, they have enough on the President, and you, to ruin both of you. ISB is like J. Edgar Hoover on steroids. They have files on everyone. And they aren't afraid to use them. You have no power over the ISB."

"What the hell are you talking about? What do they think they have on me?"

"You really want me to go into it, right now?" Chandler glanced pointedly at Cammie.

"Why are you looking at me? What are you talking about? Mom and Dad are practically saints. You know that. What could anyone have on them?"

"Let's just say that calling them saints might be a slight exaggeration and leave it at that." Chandler shrugged. There was a disparaging tone to his voice that Cammie wanted someone to explain.

"What are you talking about? Mom, what's he talking about?"

"How much do you know, Chandler?" Ronnie asked.

"I know everything." Chandler chuckled, bitterly. "Well, I hope I know everything because God help both of you, if there's more."

"What? What do you know? What's going on?" Cammie asked.

"Honey let's just leave it alone. Let Chandler finished telling us his story. We can talk to your mom and dad about their situation later." Mac rubbed his wife's shoulders as he tried to calm her down.

"So, ok then. Fine. Your mom and I aren't saints. Is that part of the reason you did this to us? Did you think we deserved to spend three years thinking you were dead? You think we're that bad? We are sinners bound for hell, so you just decided to give us an early taste of it. Was that what you were aiming for?"

"Absolutely not. In fact, well, sorry but I might as well be honest here. You had nothing to do with the decision-making process. You were collateral damage. I was sorry that it had to hurt you, but Chandler Blake needed to die, so I could have a life. I knew it was going to hurt you. I felt bad about it. But I promised Chelsea I'd clue you in when I could, and I did what I had to do."

"Collateral damage? Damn, boy. You're a piece of work. People say I can be heartless, but you take the prize." Isaiah shook his head in disbelief as he spoke.

"Senator Blake, honestly, three years was never part of the plan. I would not have agreed to it if I had known how long it was going to take." Chelsea interjected.

"Right. I thought it would all die down in a matter of months. I had planned for us to hide out in a small village in Italy. I had someone watching Chelsea. I figured the ISB would keep her under surveillance for a while… I knew they would be suspicious that my death was a ruse… but I thought if I kept my distance from her for a few months they'd give up. That's what I expected. That's what I planned. We were supposed to meet in Paris nine months after my… uhm… death. I was there when she got there, waiting for her, and I spotted four ISB agents within the first ten minutes after she arrived. They were all over her. Plus, there was a couple of Cordoba Cartel operatives following her, too. I spent a good deal of time investigating the Cordoba Cartel so, I guess they had figured out I wasn't dead, as well. She had so many eyes on her…. I couldn't even get close to her."

"Worst week of my whole life…" Chelsea said. "I was wandering around Paris waiting for Chandler to pop out of the woodwork, but he didn't. I knew ISB was there. They actually made contact with me. Warned me that someone other than ISB was also watching me. It was awful. At the end of the week, I went back home. And just waited to hear from him. I waited for two years."

"And I headed back to Italy. I was on the train, trying to come up with a different plan when I thought of plastic surgery. I realized it was the only option. I went to a doctor that was known for the kind of physical transformation I needed. It was just dumb luck that the money laundering syndicate had also contacted him, looking for someone to slide into Jean-Luc's identity."

"Are you still involve with them?"

"No, not at all. Jean-Luc had a ton of their money tied up in short term CDs. They promised me that as soon as they had their money back, I was a free man…. It took me a year and a half. I had to divest slowly to keep Interpol from asking questions. I took some record-breaking losses at the baccarat tables in Monte Carlo, but I got the job done, and when I did, they were good to their word. When they had their money back, I was in the clear. I waited a couple of months, just to make sure they weren't going to come back with a 'just one more thing' kind of deal, and when they didn't, I sent for Chelsea."

"And you don't think the ISB have any idea who you are."

"I don't." Chelsea piped in. "Honestly, the Paris trip, wandering around looking for Chandler and not finding him, was horrible, but in the grand scheme of things, it was probably the best thing that could have happened because, they followed me everywhere before that, I mean they didn't even try to disguise the fact that they were following me. And afterwards, after I met Sam. It tapered off. I think he believed me when I told him that I didn't know where Chandler was … and I guess the Cordoba Cartel figured that out, as well. They weren't interested in me, they just wanted me to lead them to Chandler and when I didn't, when they started believing I couldn't, they weren't interested in me any longer. I haven't been aware of anyone stalking me in months. Over a year, actually."

"And her senses are finally tuned to that. Very finely tuned. She knew someone was watching us the night we were kissing on the Ferris wheel. That picture you saw, Cammie. That kiss was really me, trying to calm her down. She knew someone was watching."

"And there's no other indication you're under suspicion." Isaiah asked.

"None."

"Well, we did have a peeping Tom one night." Chelsea corrected him.

Chandler shifted uncomfortably in his seat. "Yeah, that was two months ago, after we finally got back together. We live on a Cabin Cruiser at a marina in Istanbul, and Chelsea noticed someone standing on the deck of the boat, looking in the window. I tried to go after them but.... they were off the boat before I got out the door and I wasn't dressed to chase them down the dock."

Doug eyed him speculatively. "But you don't think that was related to ISB?"

"No. Not at all."

"Right, and it's only happened once." Chelsea chimed in.

"Right." Chandler agreed. "Only once."

CHAPTER TWENTY

"So about your peeper…." Doug asked later that evening, as he and Chandler stood out on the deck, overlooking the sea.

"What about it?"

"Chandler, you may have a different face, but your body language hasn't changed. I can still tell when you're not being totally forthcoming…. So, what was that all about? You obviously know more than you've told Chelsea. Do you think the ISB is on to you?"

"No, it's not the ISB. I'm sure of that." He sighed. "I just don't want to worry Chelsea…"

"You know who the peeper was, don't you?"

"Yeah, the night I went out after the peeper, she got away but not before I got a good look at her."

"Her?"

"Yeah, it's definitely a woman."

"Who do you think it is, if not ISB?"

"Someone who knew Jean-Luc, maybe? That's my guess, anyway."

Doug sighed. "Someone who knew Jean-Luc, huh? That's

the story you're going with. Some woman who knew Jean-Luc what, over two years ago, is stalking you, now?"

"It could be."

"But it's not."

"Don't tell Chelsea."

"I swear, son, it's like you wear a trouble magnet. Chandler, more secrets? You're keeping things from that girl again? Why would you do that? Has this mess taught you nothing? Why are you keeping secrets from her, again? What the hell have you gotten yourself into?"

"I don't know. The whole thing is weird."

"What whole thing?"

"Doug, after Chelsea and I didn't connect in Paris, I really didn't know if we were ever going to see each other, again. I thought I might just have to let her go… never contact her. I was determined that she was not going to come back into my life until I was certain I could keep her safe. I would never want to put her at risk, again. I took the best option available to me… I assumed Jean-Luc's identity, but I didn't know if the European syndicate would really keep their word to let me go as soon as I had returned their money. I had no idea. They could have blackmailed me for the rest of my life. And I wasn't going to pull Chelsea back into it again if there was any chance of her being put back in a dangerous situation. I missed her. A lot. More than I even thought I would. It was a troubled time. I was depressed. I had a new face and was trying to be a new person. I didn't know if I was going to be able to pull it off…"

"And…"

"And I spent several months in the hospital. The doctor, the plastic surgeon that helped with the ruse, said it was necessary. My surgery scars healed within a couple of months, but the injuries that Jean-Luc had were extensive. I mean, let's get real, he was dead when they pulled him out of that car. He was injured so badly that he died, man. I mean, people got him out of the car after the wreck. They saw what a mess he was in.... if he had survived, it would have taken a long time for him to recover... so I had to stay in the hospital... go through all kinds of therapy... as part of the ruse. It was a good respite, in that, it gave me time to really study up on Jean-Luc. I knew the man well, by the time I got out... but it was a very lonely time."

"Lonely?" Doug sighed. "Chandler and lonely is never a good combination."

"No...There was a nurse..."

"A nurse?"

"Yeah, we had a fling."

"How long did this fling last?"

"About four months."

"What happened?"

"I realized she was taking it all too seriously, so I ended it."

"How'd she take that?"

"Not well..."

"What happened?"

"She tried to stab me with an ice pick."

"Obviously, she didn't succeed."

"No. I managed to wrestle it out of her hands. I told her I wouldn't press charges, but I never wanted to see her again."

"Does she know who you really are?"

"No."

"But she knows you're not really Jean-Luc?"

"No. She has no idea." After my plastic surgery scars were healed, I went to a convalescence home... as Jean-Luc. She was a nurse on the floor. She told me she had always had a crush on me, well, on Jean-Luc. She was a big racing fan. That's how it started. She would talk to me about my races. I got a lot of information from her by telling her that I was having trouble remembering the races. She was happy to fill me in. She would sneak in snacks and things for me. Come in and spend some time with me after her shift was over. She totally bought the story that I had some memory issues because of the brain damage. So, she spent a lot of time helping me remember things. We spent a lot of time together. Things happen. We had a fling."

"In the hospital."

"Yeah, and when I was finally released. I told her I was going back to my home in Istanbul to finish my recuperation. She wanted to come with me. I told her that she didn't need to quit her job for me. I gave her the speech about how I wasn't ready for a long-term relationship before the accident… certainly not now, with me still recuperating. In my defense, it wasn't the first time I had told her that. I thought she understood that it wasn't a forever thing, but I guess she had imagined things would go differently. She got really angry. Said I used her."

"And you thought that was the end of it?"

"Yeah, until about a month later, I was out running with one of my neighbors at the marina. He and Jean-Luc had been big buddies, and when I came home, so to speak, he expected the friendship to continue. He's a good guy. I like him, so… it's not a problem to spend time with him. We still run together."

"So, something happened with the girl?"

"Yeah, we came back to my boat for a beer one night after running, and she had broken in. She was ripping up the upholstery, in my, well, Jean-Luc's sofas with an ice pick. She came at me. I managed to wrestle it out of her hands. I told her that I had better not see her again or I would press charges against her."

"And you had a witness to this."

"Yeah…" Chandler sighed.

"And you haven't seen her since?"

"Not really sure. It was definitely her that night with Chelsea. Before that, there had been a couple of times, that I thought I caught a glimpse of her--- like in a crowded bar, or once, I was on my, Jean-Luc's, bike, and a city bus pulled up beside me. A woman was sitting in the bus, she was staring at me out the window. I think it was her, but she turned her head away quickly and I couldn't be sure.

There have been several things like that, but they were all just fleeting impressions. I told myself, it was my imagination. Or a guilty conscience, maybe. But I was suspicious that she was still in Istanbul. Part of the reason I put off contacting Chelsea. I waited several months after I paid off the syndicate. I wanted to make sure there was no additional demands on their part and I wanted to make sure that Juliette was gone. Then when there were no more problems, I sent for Chelsea.

When she got to Istanbul, I didn't contact her for over a month. Still, no sign of Juliette at all. No sign of the ISB either. So, I thought we were safe. Salvatore, my neighbor, in the marina, the one who was with me the night we found her ransacking the boat… he told me a few days ago, he thought he had seen her on the dock one night a couple of weeks back, like me, he wasn't sure. Otherwise, the only time I'm sure I've seen her is the night she was watching us."

"Well, maybe she's gone, maybe she's still lurking about… but, Chandler, either way, you need to be honest with Chelsea."

"I tried. I absolutely tried. She asked me if there had been other women and I told her that there were times when I was lonely. I admitted that sometimes I went out and found someone to ease the loneliness. She was understanding, but it broke her heart. I could see it in her eyes. I've hurt her so much and, there I was, hurting her again. I just didn't want to hurt her, anymore. I told her that there had been women, but they were all one-night stands and that seemed to make it easier for her… and it wasn't a total lie. I don't feel like I had a relationship with Juliette. It was, as far as I was concerned, nothing more than a series of one-night stands. They just happened to be with the same woman."

"Chandler." Doug raised his eyebrows judgmentally.

"I know. I screwed up. Big time. Not the first time. Probably won't be the last… although I promise you, I won't cheat on Chelsea. Damn, Doug, we were apart for three years. It was the longest three years of my life. I mean, I never loved anyone else… But… I'm not a saint. And, I'm being honest, it was nothing more to me than a one-night stand… it really wasn't even like I was cheating on Chelsea, because there was never, not one second, when I would not have preferred to be with her. Juliette and the others were always second choice."

Doug chuckled. "I'm going to make a wild guess here that Chelsea might not see it that way."

"I know. That's why I don't want to tell her." Chandler responded morosely. "But that's the way I saw it. I promise. There's not a doubt in my mind, if I could have been with Chelsea, I would have never even looked at those other women."

"I believe that." Doug conceded. "But you need to understand…you have a good woman. I kept up with her while you were gone. She was as loyal to you as she could possibly be. Your parents were ugly to her at the beginning. They thought she was responsible for your suicide. Then they decided they wanted to be close to her because she was a link to you. They wouldn't leave her alone. There were days when your mother was calling her five or six times a day. And she put up with all of it. I talked to her a few months ago, and I'll tell you the truth, it had been so long since we heard from you that I thought you were probably dead… I thought you were dead, and I wanted to go ahead and tell your parents the truth. I thought they deserved to know. She convinced me to wait a few more months. She told me she still believed you were out there… somewhere. Said she thought she would know it, feel it, if you were gone. She believed you were still alive, and she convinced me to wait for a few more months to protect you… She loves you so much. You won't ever find another woman like that. Not in your lifetime. And I don't want to see you blow it. "

"I know." Chandler agreed. "She's been great. She's put up with more than any woman should ever have to put up with, and I'm going to do better."

"You need to, because you're right…. She's great. A real gem. But there's only so much any woman is going to put up with and, son, I think you've maxed out here. You can't keep piling it on and expect her to hang in there forever. You'll end up losing this girl if…"

"There is no if. I'm not going to do anything to lose her. Doug, I love her. I missed her every moment of every day when we were apart. I was miserable, lonely. We were apart almost three years. I made some mistakes. Some big mistakes. I don't deny that… but those mistakes were made because I missed her so much…. now that we are together, I'm not going to…. Damn, I don't even want another woman. She's the only woman I will ever want. So, you don't have to worry. "

"I hope not... because she's the best thing that's ever happened to you, and if you blow this...."

"That's one thing you don't have to worry about. I promise. I'm not ever going to hurt Chelsea, again." Chandler proclaimed adamantly, but the expression on Doug's face indicated he was not convinced.

"You know...." Isaiah said as he walked out on the deck to join them. "I've put up with you monopolizing my son's life, for most of his life... Good Old' Uncle Doug." His tone was teasing but with an underlying bitterness. "I was busy with my career and I was always grateful for the time you spent with Chandler when I didn't have that time, but right now, it seems just a little bit too selfish."

"Sorry." Doug said. "We just walked out for some fresh air. You're welcomed to join us."

"Thanks. I think I'll take you up on that." He muttered, the bitterness more apparent. "Chandler, I've been thinking. For the time being, I think you're going to have to continue playing Jean-Luc. You are safer that way right now. I'm going to put my staff to investigating ISB as soon as I get back to DC, but until we can bring them down, I think...."

"Whoa! Stop. Slow down. What the hell are you talking about?" Chandler asked.

"I'm talking about you resuming your rightful name, so you can get on with your real life. We're going to bring ISB down. What you've told me is unacceptable."

"No. We're not going to bring ISB down. You couldn't bring ISB down if you tried. You'll end up dead and I don't want to be responsible for that. You've got to promise me, dad, you can't do anything. You can't say anything. You can't fix this. And I don't want you to even try."

"Chandler, somehow you've never fully been able to

understand this, but I have infinite resources at hand. When I tell the majority leader what's been going on…"

"You're not going to tell anyone." Chandler snapped.

"Of course, I'm going to tell people. Do you know how hard this has been on your mother and me? Having people think our only son committed suicide? You're damned right we are going to tell people it wasn't true. You are a hero. You've served your country with honor and sacrificed more than anyone should ever be asked to sacrifice."

"And no one is ever going to know about it. They can't."

"Of course they can. And I'm going to see to it they do." Isaiah said. His voice angry and obstinate.

"No, you're not." Chandler was also angry.

"OK, you two. Calm down." Doug said, touching both on the shoulders in an attempt to bring peace. "This is a wonderful day for our family. Let's not ruin it with an argument. We can talk about this later."

"There's nothing to talk about." Chandler insisted. "He's not going to tell anyone."

"Well, what the hell do you think you're going to do? Just stay Jean-Luc for the rest of your life?" Isaiah asked.

"That's the plan. Yeah."

"So are you just planning on cutting your mother and me out of your life, again. I mean you can't take back your rightful place in our family as long as people think you're dead. Don't you think people are going to wonder why Jean-Luc Moreau comes to our house for Christmas?"

"You're close to Chelsea. She'll visit you. I'll be with her."

"That's not good enough. I want people to know my son is not some coward who took his own life."

"Well, dad, I hate to break it to you, but we don't always get what we want."

"I can bring these people down."

"And put Chelsea, Cameron, her little girl, Mom, me, yourself… all of us… in danger's way. Just so you won't be embarrassed by your cowardly, suicidal son. No. You're not going to do it."

"Chandler, I hate to break it to you, but you are not the final authority on what I say or do."

"No, I'm not. I can't control you. I know that. But you need to know this. If you start investigating the ISB, if you stir things up, I'll have no choice but to disappear, again. Do you get that? I will have to go back under deep cover. And this time I'll be gone for good."

"What's going on out here?" Veronica asked as she walked out on the deck, followed by Chelsea and Cammie. "You two can't be arguing again already."

"We're not arguing. I'm just trying to talk some sense into your son. He actually thinks he's going to be Jean-Luc Moreau for the rest of his life."

"I don't have a choice."

"You do. I can form a committee and…"

"Put the whole family in danger. No. I mean this, dad. If you don't leave this alone, Chelsea and I will have to go underground. You won't ever see us again."

"Isaiah… please. We lost him once. Now, we have him back… You can't do anything that makes him leave again. Please." Ronnie pleaded, digging her long pink nails into her husband's arm.

"No one is even going to know who he is." Isaiah's voice was trembling. "He's a hero. My son is the hero I knew he could be, and no one is ever going to know. I can't stand the thoughts of that. It is asking too much. People need to know what he's done. Chandler, the world needs to know what you've sacrificed."

"We know, daddy." Came said. "This is not a perfect situation. It's not ideal. No one is saying that it is. But we have him back. No matter what name he goes by, we have Chandler back. It's like a miracle. Just think about us yesterday, or a week ago. We were so upset about making this trip, meeting Chelsea's new love. It was almost more than we could stand. And here we are, just a few days later, with Chandler. He's here. With us. We couldn't have even imagined this yesterday. We would have agreed to anything to have him back. And now we have him. You can't make him go away, again."

"I don't like this." Isaiah growled. "This is not right."

"It's more right than anything we've known in the past three years when we thought we would never see him again…" Veronica said.

"Daddy, please." Cammie pleaded.

Isaiah sighed. "I don't like this. I don't like anything about it."

"It's not my first choice, either." Chandler explained, his voice calm once again. "This is not the way I wanted Chelsea and I to live our lives. But we've adjusted. You will, too."

CHAPTER TWENTY-ONE

"Everyone is settled into their rooms." Chelsea smiled, walking into the bedroom she was sharing with Chandler. He was sitting on the bed. Legs stretched out, back against the headboard. Shirtless. He reached out for her.

"Come here." he said, pulling her down beside him. He kissed her, slowly, seductively, passionately as he pushed her down onto the mattress.

"Wow. What was that for?" Chelsea asked, breathless.

"It's for being the most wonderful woman in the world."

"Are you just now figuring that out?" she teased.

"No, I already knew. But it was reinforced by Uncle Doug tonight. I got quite a lecture from him. He said you were the best thing that ever happened to me and I better not screw it up."

"I love your Uncle Doug."

"He loves you, too."

"What did you say to that?"

"I said I already knew how wonderful you are." He smiled, pulling her into his arms for another deep kiss.

After a minute, she pulled away, reluctantly. "I really need to take a shower." She smiled. "Wanna join me?"

"Damn right I do." Chandler enthused.

She took his hand and led him into the ceramic and glass shower stall. The shower head in the ceiling sent a thick, heavy stream of steamy hot water over their bodies as Chandler pressed her against the tiled wall. His lips on her face, her neck, her shoulders, her breasts, as her hands ran up and down his muscular arms. For just a moment, life seemed perfect. They were together. Chandler's family knew the truth. It had been a long and difficult road, but, in Chelsea's mind, at least, they had made it. They had finally found their happily ever after.

CHAPTER TWENTY-TWO

They stayed for ten days in Amasra. There was laughter, there were tears, there were arguments. But through it all, Chelsea recognized, for the first time how much love there was in the Blake family. During the time they believed he was dead; she had come to realize how deeply his family loved him. Now she understood that he loved them, as well.

Little Chandler, Cameron's daughter, had been left in L.A., with her paternal grandparents. But, once Cammie realized her brother was alive, she was determined that he would meet his namesake. On the second day of their visit, Mac flew back to Los Angeles. An eighteen-hour flight, and three days later, he returned with the young child, a beautiful blue-eyed blonde, who bonded immediately with her uncle. Chelsea watched with delight as he spent hour upon hour playing games with his newly discovered niece.

"You're going to make a wonderful daddy." Chelsea told him later that night, when they were alone in their room. "Someday… when the time is right."

"Do you ever think about our baby?" Chandler asked.

They had not discussed the miscarriage since they had been reconciled. Not even once.

"I think about her every day. She'd be almost four now. I think she would look a lot like Baby Chandler. At least that's how I imagine her."

"She?"

"Yeah, she. I never had any doubt she was a little girl. It was too early for the doctor to determine the sex, but I've always thought about her as a her. When little Chandler was born, I was even more sure of it. They would have been best friends, I think." She smiled sadly, tears springing to her eyes. "I can imagine them playing dolls together, running from the waves down on the beach where your parents live. She would have been several months older, so she would have probably been bossy. But they would have loved one another. Just like you and Cammie love one another."

"I think so too." He paused for a moment. "You know, we can't fix that. That's a void we can never fill. But we can give little Chandler a younger friend…"

"You want to have another baby?" Chelsea asked, surprised. "Like now? You want to have another baby?"

"I'd like that. But, no, not yet. I want to wait until everything is right, perfect. The day you lost the baby, the doctor said that a genetic defect was the most likely reason for a miscarriage so early in the pregnancy, nature's way of taking care of a mistake. That's how he described it. But I've never been sure that was true. We were both under so much stress at the time… I put you under so much stress… I'll always wonder…. I don't want to risk that, again. I want us to have another baby; but not until you can just be happy, and carefree, and concentrate on getting fat, and satisfying all your weird cravings."

"How did you know about my weird cravings… I never

told you."

"I thought about it a lot, after… after you went back to Mississippi. You had a banana popsicle in your hand every single minute of the day for several weeks before the miscarriage."

Chelsea laughed. "Yeah, banana popsicles were a definite craving. And marshmallows. I think I ate about ten bags of marshmallows."

"I didn't know about the marshmallows."

"I'm sorry I didn't tell you."

"So am I. I understand. I've always understood. But I wish I could have put my hand on your stomach and told it, well, ok, told her, that I loved her. Just once."

"I did that for both of us." Chelsea laughed for a moment then her smile faded. "But you don't think it's safe to try, again?"

"Not yet."

"Do you still think the ISB might be on to you? Tell me the truth Chandler, I need to know."

"Chelsea, I am telling you the truth. I don't think the ISB has a clue that I'm Jean-Luc. I don't think they are on to us. Not at all."

"Then I don't understand why you don't think it's safe."

"I just want everything to be perfect. And, honestly, I promise you, I think we are almost there." Chandler pulled her into his arms. "Let's just give it a few more months."

"OK. A few more months it is." She cuddled against his bare chest and sighed contentedly, trying hard to ignore the tiny doubts that were dancing through her thoughts. What were they waiting for? He wanted to wait until things were perfect. She thought they already were. What was worrying him? What was holding him back? What was he not telling her?

CHAPTER TWENTY-THREE

If only things could stay like this forever, Chelsea thought, at least a million times during the next few days. But, of course, life moved on. After saying a bitter-sweet good-bye to the Blake family, Chandler and Chelsea returned to Istanbul, to continue with their happily ever after. And, for a while, things were blissful. As far as Chelsea knew.

She loved her job. Her students were bright and inquisitive. And with only fourteen in her class, she had ample time to experiment with all the creative procedures that teachers serving a hundred or more a day could only imagine… this was truly a dream job.

She had made true friends in Chloe, Charlotte, and Miranda. She was completely happy with Chandler. In the future, she would think of their life together in Istanbul, as the happiest in her life. But there was always a little something in the back of her brain, a nagging little thought, eating away at her, warning her that something was not quite right.

The weeks passed by quickly. Christmas, they learned, was not a big deal in Istanbul. The streets and store windows were decorated with lights and trees, in anticipation of New Years, though, and with a large, expatriated community of Westerners, there were numerous restaurants and nightclubs which offered traditional holiday entertainment. But there were very few places to buy Christmas decorations and live fir trees were exceptionally hard to find.

Chelsea ordered decorations from the internet, in hopes they would arrive before Christmas, and on the twenty-third, when she came home from school, she was delighted to see a live Christmas tree in the living area of their boat.

Chandler had learned of a tree lot on the outskirts of the city and driven there to pick it up. They spent the afternoon decorating it, as they drank hot chocolate and told stories about favorite Christmas holidays from their past.

On Christmas Eve, they attended midnight mass at the Church of St. Anthony of Padua, the largest Roman Catholic Church in Istanbul; Chandler's suggestion had surprised Chelsea. He had never shown a lot of interest in religion, but he insisted that mass on Christmas Eve was necessary. At the service they ran into their marina neighbors, Charles and Aletha Lansing, Australians by birth, and after the service was finished, they found a cozy all-night bar where they drank champagne and celebrated the season.

On Christmas morning, Chelsea awoke to a heavy rainfall. And a small package on Chandler's pillow.

"Open me." A note on the card said.

"Chandler, where are you?" Chelsea called out. There was no answer, so she quickly opened the package. To her surprise there was a beautiful emerald ring in the box.

"Like it?" Chandler asked. Standing in the doorway.

"It's beautiful. It's the most beautiful ring I've ever seen." Chelsea choked.

"Good. I know diamonds are traditional, but I went with

the emeralds because… well, you seem to have an affection for the color green."

"Yeah, your beautiful green eyes. I miss them. But I've gotten used to the brown."

"I can't ever be green-eyed Chandler again. You know that. So, I thought I'd go with the emerald, so you'd never forget who you are really married to."

"Married?"

"That's what I said." He smiled. One of the few times Chelsea had ever seen him appear to be almost shy. "This is an engagement ring. I think it's time we get married. Move back to the states, give little Chandler a best friend. You know, get on with the whole happily ever after thing. How do you feel about that idea?"

Chelsea's eyes filled with tears. "I love that idea." She threw her arms around his neck and kissed him. "But baby… are you sure? I mean, it's too soon isn't it?"

"Too soon? We've been in love for four years. I know people who have met, fallen in love, married, divorced and done it all again in less time than that."

"Chandler and Chelsea have been in love for four years." She reminded him, suddenly cautious and a little fearful about taking this next big step. "Jean-Luc and Chelsea have known each other three months. What will people think if we get married, or even engaged, this soon. I don't want you to blow your cover"

"No. I've given this some thought, and, actually, I think it works well with my cover story. Jean-Luc was known for being impulsive. If he wanted something, he went for it. If he wanted to do something, he did it. I think the people who knew him will believe that once he found the woman he wanted to spend his life with, he wanted to get on with that life. It's a very Jean-Luc thing to do. So, we get engaged.

After we marry, you can finish your school term and then we can move back to the states. I'm thinking maybe North Carolina. How does that sound to you?"

"North Carolina? Why North Carolina?"

"I don't think we can go back to California. If ISB is still watching, that might be a little too obvious. But I, well, Chandler, has no ties to North Carolina. It's a day's drive from Washington where Mom and Dad are. It's a day's drive from Violet Springs where your family are. I'll tell people that I'm being nudged toward driving again… which is the truth… I've heard from quite a few of Jean-Luc's racing buddies in the last couple of months, and they all think I should hit the circuit, again. I can say I don't want to race anymore. Tell people the idea makes me nervous. And the pressure is causing panic attacks. I just want a quiet, peaceful life. You can find a teaching job in North Carolina. And, Chelsea, I think I'm going to go back to school."

"School?"

"Yeah, school. After what happened at Stanfield, I went to quite a few different schools. University of South Florida, Harvard, Duke, University of Houston, Columbia. I was always on assignment. When the assignment was finished, I left. So, I never finished. But I really liked Duke. Good school. I'll have to start from the beginning. Jean-Luc did not go to college. But I'll probably take it more seriously, now, anyway, so, it'll be good for me."

"What will you study?"

"Not sure. Chandler was majoring in Political Science. I planned on following in my dad's footsteps at one time. Still, something I'm interested in but that's another thing that might be a little too much to explain away as a coincidence. So, I'm thinking maybe journalism. With Jean-Luc's celebrity status, maybe I could get a job as a television news commentator."

"Are you serious?"

"Not really. Not about being a commentator. But yes, I'm serious about school. So, what do you think? Is the idea of being a southern schoolteacher with a husband in college too plebeian for you, now that you've played cloak and dagger and seen the world?"

"I think it sounds like the most wonderful life in the entire world." Chelsea exclaimed, honestly. "I think it sounds perfect. Absolutely perfect." She threw her arms around his neck and kissed him. Then, after gently sliding the ring on her finger, it was a perfect fit, he pushed her back down on the bed and they spent the rest of Christmas Day making love.

CHAPTER TWENTY-FOUR

On New Years' Eve, they arranged to celebrate with their friends at The Emerald Club, the place where they had first met as Jean-Luc and Chelsea. Charles and Aletha, neighbors from the dock, as well as Chloe, Charlotte, Miranda, and their dates, were all there to join into the celebration. Ajax, who by this time, had broken up with Charlotte, made an appearance with a blonde model. Several of Jean-Luc's crew were also in attendance. And Chelsea Face Timed Cammie and Mac, back in the states, as they made the announcement.

As predicted, people expressed surprise at the suddenness of the engagement. "You've only known each other a few months." Charlotte said, trying, without success, to keep the disapproving tone from her voice.

"Man, when you had that wreck, they said you had brain damage but other than the memory problems you seemed so normal afterwards I didn't believe it. Now I'm not so sure." Ajax teased.

"Never thought I'd see the day." Gregor, Jean-Luc's pit-crew chief, shook his head in disbelief.

"Chelsea, you know we want you to be happy but, are you sure this is not too soon?" Chloe asked.

"No. I'm one hundred percent certain it's fine." She vowed, and then, with an answer that she had thought of in advance. "You know, when I lost Chandler, I realized that none of us are guaranteed tomorrow. I didn't know if I would ever find true love again. But I did. And now that I have it, I don't want to waste a minute of it."

"Yeah, and, I'm on the other side of that." Chandler joined in with an answer he and Chelsea had also practiced. "I almost died in Germany. The day I hit that wall, I almost died. Now that I know how precious life is, I want to enjoy every moment of it to the max… and I've come to realize I'm happiest when I'm with Chelsea. So, yeah, it's soon. But for us, it's right." He spoke with a certainty no one could argue with as he took her hand in his and kissed it gently.

"Well, ok, then." Ajax shrugged. "I guess we need to order a bottle of champagne… maybe about three. We have more than a new year to celebrate."

"I want to see that ring, again." Charlotte said, later in the evening, when she and Chelsea were in the ladies' room. "Girl, I can't believe this is happening. Dang. You just come to Istanbul, and in less than a month, you find yourself a husband. A hot sexy race car driver, no less. Some girls have all the luck."

"You're getting married?" A woman turned from the lavatory mirror and looked speculatively at her. It was a familiar face. Not someone Chelsea knew, but someone she had seen several times before in places like the food market, a favorite dress shop, walking on the dock.

"Yes. I am." Chelsea said proudly holding up her ring. "I got engaged on Christmas morning."

"Congratulations. I'm impressed. I didn't think Jean-Luc would ever settle down. You must be some kind of magician.... Or really special in bed. Maybe you should write a book. Give the rest of us some tips." Chelsea noticed immediately that the woman's smile did not reach her eyes.

"Excuse me." The sexual innuendo from a stranger was extremely inappropriate in Chelsea's eyes and the sharp tone of her voice conveyed those feelings.

"Oh, don't get all bent out of shape. I'm just wondering how you pulled this off. Jean-Luc and I had fabulous sex and he certainly wasn't interested in marrying me. I'm Juliette, by the way. I'm sure you've never heard of me, just like the next girl will never hear of you. Not from Jean-Luc, at least. When he's done with a woman, he's done."

Chelsea smiled her biggest, brightest fake smile. She was unsure of exactly how to respond. The woman was attractive. Her hair was a dark ebony, and with dark eyeliner, thick false eyelashes, and ruby red lips, she looked like a goth. Not at all Chandler's type, but Chelsea reminded herself, this woman didn't know Chandler. And more importantly, Chandler didn't know her.

This was undoubtedly, one of Jean-Luc's, the real Jean-Luc's, former lovers. It was awkward but, at that particular moment, it was not at all distressing... she had met women who had slept with Jean-Luc before, it was bound to happen again, she told herself. Given his reputation with the ladies it would probably happen many times. And, it had nothing to do with her relationship with Chandler. Still, it was a tricky situation. She had no idea what the appropriate response should be. Jealous? Smug? Condescending? How would she react if she met a former lover of Chandler's, she asked herself… and that guided her response.

"Evidently there have been a lot of women in Jean-Luc's past. He hasn't ever tried to hide that from me. He's told me that he was a different person before the accident than he is now…." Chelsea smiled kindly. No need to be rude or condescending. "He wasn't interested at all in settling down then, but since the wreck… he's changed a lot."

"Sweetie, it wasn't the wreck that changed him." There was a broad smile on her face as she spoke, but she spat out the words in a way that indicated anger, controlled anger, but anger, nonetheless.

"He and I hooked up while he was still at the hospital after the wreck. He wasn't interested in settling down then, either. I thought he was… but I was wrong. He completely fooled me, and I don't fool easily. So, all I can say, is watch yourself with him. He didn't give me a ring, but he gave me every reason to believe he would, someday. I thought he loved me, he told me he did and I believed him. He made me feel like I was the most special woman in the world and then when he was done with me, he threw me out of his life like I was used up trash. So, just a warning, girl to girl…. Be careful. Don't let him break your heart. He's more than capable of it. In fact, I think he kind of gets off on it." She applied her lipstick, winked encouragingly at Chelsea, and then walked, flounced was a better word for it, out of the bathroom, slamming the door behind her.

"Well, how rude." Charlotte said when the door slammed shut. "Chelsea, don't pay any attention to her. You can look at her and know Jean-Luc never cared for her. She may not even be telling the truth about…."

Charlotte's voice trailed off as Chelsea considered what the girl had said. *"An affair while he was in the hospital."*

Chandler had admitted to having had sex, one night stands he called them, during the time they were apart. That had broken her heart, but she had accepted it. This sounded different, though. This sounded like a relationship.

"Just don't mention this to Jean-Luc." Chelsea told Charlotte as they made their way back to the table.

"Are you not going to tell him about it?"

"Yeah, I'm going to tell him. I'd just rather have the conversation in private. So, don't mention it. Please." Chelsea pleaded.

"Ok, but honestly Chelsea, I wouldn't worry about it for two minutes. Jean-Luc didn't even know you, then. If he had, I'm sure, he wouldn't have given her a second glance."

If only, Chelsea thought.... If only that were true.

They rejoined their dates at the table, and spent the rest of the evening dancing, but Chelsea's heart was not in it. Had he really told another woman he loved her while she was sitting in Mississippi wondering if she would ever hear from him again? She didn't even want to know the answer. But she needed to know. She had to know.

"Are you ok?" Chandler asked at least five times during the evening.

"I'm just tired." Chelsea responded.

"Are you sure?"

"We'll talk about it when we get home." She snapped.

"So, there is an *it* to talk about...."

"Yes, there is definitely an it." She conceded, trying hard to keep the anger out of her voice. "And we will talk about it when we get home."

An icy rain was falling when they left The Emerald Club shortly after two o'clock on New Year's morning. Chandler put his arm around her, pulling her close as they walked toward the Uber ride. She stiffened, involuntarily pulling away.

"Chelsea, what the hell is wrong with you tonight?"

"I said that we will talk about it when we get home…" she wanted to be able to look at his face, look into his eyes, when she told him what the woman, Juliette, had said. She didn't think he would lie to her, but if Juliette's story was true, he had already lied… so she wanted to see his face when she gave him the chance to confirm or deny the affair.

The ride back to the marina was quiet and uncomfortable, but that changed when they walked down the dock toward their boat slip.

"What the hell?"

"Chandler, I told you…"

"I'm not worried about your bad mood, right now. Look at the boat."

Chelsea's eyes grew wide with terror. It appeared the sliding glass doors that led from the deck into the main cabin had been bashed in.

"Stay here." Chandler told her as he carefully opened the door and stepped inside. Chelsea followed close behind. There might be someone waiting for them on the inside. She knew this. But she felt safer inside with Chandler than she felt waiting outside, alone.

The sofas had been ripped to shreds and the words FUCK YOU JEAN-LUC had been painted on the wall above the fireplace, as well as on the hardwood floors, with what looked to be lipstick.

In the bedroom, several of Chelsea's sweaters had been taken out and ripped into shreds. Dishes had been taken from the cabinets and bashed on the floor.

"What happened? Who did this? Why would anyone do this?" Chelsea asked. But she knew the answer and she could tell by the expression on Chandler's face that he knew, as well.

It was after six o'clock in the morning before the Polis left the boat. Chandler and Chelsea were both exhausted, but the boat was not livable, so they called a cab and ended up at a luxury hotel approximately a mile away.

Inside their room, Chelsea quickly stripped out of her party dress, washed her face, and climbed into bed, wearing nothing but a t-shirt and panties. Chandler was already there.

"Do you think this was random violence?" The Polis had suggested that sometimes on New Year's Eve, people wreaked this type of havoc.

"No. I don't think so." Chandler replied.

"Do you think the ISB…?"

"Absolutely not. This is not their modus operandi."

"So…. Who?"

"I don't know." He was hesitant. Struggling with the words. He knew who had wrecked their home, and he knew Chelsea needed to know as well. She needed to be warned.

Chelsea took a deep breath. "Chandler, is there any chance it was Juliette? She found out we are engaged tonight… She didn't look happy. Do you think it could have been her?"

"How the hell did you know about Juliette?"

"She introduced herself in the ladies' room tonight. Charlotte was inspecting my ring at the time…." Chelsea didn't even try to blink back the tears. "You lied to me."

"Chelsea…. I…"

"Don't try to make excuses. You lied to me. I know it. So, do you. You lied to me."

"I'm sorry, baby." Chandler said, his voice full of remorse.

"Yeah, me too." There was a level of bitterness in her

voice that he had not heard before. "I mean I guess, in the grand scheme of things, it doesn't really matter all that much. Whether you screwed a hundred girls, or you screwed one girl a hundred times…. I mean, I guess it doesn't really matter… Either way, I was in Mississippi praying you'd send for me… just praying somehow we could be together again, and you were getting off every time you got a chance."

"Chelsea, it wasn't like that."

"Well, what was it like… please tell me. What was it like? Cause I really want to know."

"You are the only woman I have ever loved. You have to know that."

"Did you tell Juliette she was the only woman you ever loved, too? Is that what you say to every woman?"

"No. Absolutely not. I have never said those words to another woman."

"Juliette said you told her you loved her. She thought the two of you would end up getting married."

"That's a lie."

"You never told Juliette you were in love with her?"

"No. You're the only woman I've ever said those words to, and you have to know that. Tell me that you know that?"

"I guess I do know. Honestly, that's the worst part of it. I do know you love me as much or more than you have ever loved anyone. But even so… you have no problem jumping on whatever is available if I'm not there. And you have no problem lying to me about it. You love me, but let's get real, here… love just doesn't seem to mean to you what it does to me."

"That's not true."

"So why is there a Juliette? There's not a John, or a Jimmy or a Jack. Because I love you. I was lonely while we were apart, too, Chandler. I was lonely, and miserable, and I have needs, too. But I needed you. I didn't need John, or Jimmy or Jack. So why is there a Juliette? If you love me the same way that I love you, why is there a Juliette? Just explain that to me. Please. I really want to understand."

"Cause you're the best person in the world. And I know that. I've always known it. I told you, when we met, before we hooked up, I told you, I wasn't good enough for you. You argued with me, but I did warn you… and Chelsea, I'm so grateful there wasn't a John, or a Jimmy or Jack. That would have broken my heart…."

"Juliette broke my heart."

"I get that. And I have no excuse. All I can tell you is that I was miserable. I didn't know if we were ever going to be able to get together again, or not. I was backed into a corner. I was worried the people I made the deal with would not release me when I returned their money. I told you that. I didn't want to be Jean-Luc, but I couldn't be Chandler anymore. I was messed up, and she was there…"

"Story of your life."

"Chelsea..."

"It's true. You don't go out and chase these women down. They just appear out of nowhere and you think like, well, why not…. Is that what you thought when I just turned up with lunch one day when you were drumming on the boulevard?"

"Chelsea, no. I love you. I loved you the first moment I laid eyes on you. You are the center of my universe. Baby, you know that."

"Stop telling me what I know, Chandler. I don't know anything right now. I know what you say. But I also know that your actions belie your words. So, I don't know what to think, what to believe, anymore. I don't know what is true and what is not. All I know is that you came up with this horrible fake your own death plan so we could be together. I spent three years alone. I suffered, your parents suffered, your sister suffered, and you were screwing around the whole time. I couldn't move on with my life because I knew you were out there, somewhere. All I could do is wait. So, great! We're together now, but what happens, if we have to spend some time apart. What the hell are you going to do if I go into the hospital to have your baby? Can you spend a night alone?"

"Chelsea, I love you…"

"Stop saying that like it's a cure-all for everything. It's not. I get it… you love me. But Chandler you don't love me enough to be faithful to me. Not when we're apart. I'm not sure that really is love. Right now, I am not sure you even know what love is. And I'm too tired to argue about it anymore. I need to rest. We can talk some more tomorrow. Just move over to your side of the bed and please, don't touch me. I just don't want you to touch me right now." Those were her final words as she turned on her side, away from Chandler, and pulled the sheet over her head.

CHAPTER TWENTY-FIVE

She slept fitfully and awoke to the sound of several male voices, Chandler's included.

She showered and dressed before going into the living area of their hotel suite, where she found Chandler alone.

"I love you." He said as she walked into the room.

"Don't start with me." She was still angry.

"I said I love you."

"And I said don't start that with me right now. OK?" she sighed. "I heard voices when I first woke up?"

"The Polis came for a follow-up report?"

"Did you tell them who you think did it?"

"No. I said I thought it was random."

"How gallant of you, protecting your former lover?"

"Protecting myself."

"From what? She's already destroyed our home. If she's gunning for you then she's far less likely to get to you if she's in jail."

"You don't understand."

Chelsea groaned, loudly. "There's something you still haven't told me, isn't there?"

"Yeah." He answered reluctantly.

"SOOO… what else is it? Are you still seeing her?"

"Of course not."

"So what?"

"Chelsea, I love you."

She groaned loudly, placing her hands on either side of her head. "Stop saying that. Just stop. I'm so sick of hearing those words. I don't want to hear that from you for a long time."

"No, you have to hear it, because that's what I haven't told you. I love you. You were miserable in Mississippi without me. I was miserable without you too. You had hope I would eventually send for you and we could be back together. I didn't know if that was ever going to happen. After Paris, when I saw how intense the ISB surveillance was, I didn't know if we would ever make it. That's why I agreed to be Jean-Luc. I thought, well, at least, we'll have a chance, but lying in that hospital bed, recovering from plastic surgery, I had plenty of time to think about the whole situation. I worried that we might not ever be back together. Do you get that? I was miserable, too. I've never been more unhappy in my entire life. Juliette had a celebrity crush on Jean-Luc. She thought I was Jean-Luc. She was aggressive."

"Oh, poor Chandler. He couldn't fight off the horny nurse." Sarcasm dripping with every word Chelsea spoke.

"That's not what I'm saying."

"So, what are you saying?"

"We had sex… numerous times…." He sighed. "And a couple of times… a couple of times I accidentally called her Chelsea. One night, as I was, you know… finishing… I said the words. I said I love you, Chelsea. You asked me if I ever told her I loved her. I said the words while we were having sex. But I said them to you. Not to her. She just heard what she wanted to hear."

"You called her my name?"

"Yeah, three times, maybe four. I think the fourth time is when I said I love you. She complained the first three times, she didn't say anything the fourth... she was too happy about the I love you to worry about what name I called her."

Chelsea stared at him intently for a moment, then, with more anger than she had ever imagined she could feel, she stomped across the room and punched him hard in the stomach causing him to bend over, groaning in agony.

"You son of a bitch. That's just as insulting as hell. That's the most insulting thing anyone has ever said to me. You're a true asshole. And I, well, ok, yeah, ok I definitely understand why you didn't tell me that, but why didn't you tell the Polis..."

"I didn't tell the Polis because Jean-Luc didn't know Chelsea when he slept with Juliette. Jean-Luc and Chelsea met four months ago at a club here in Istanbul. Remember? When I left France, after the surgery, when I ended it with her, she asked me if I was going back to Chelsea? Now, I'm with Chelsea. Engaged to Chelsea. If she gets arrested, if she gets tried, she's probably going to tell her side of the story. Big, bad Jean-Luc screwing her, then going back to his true love... Chelsea., the woman that the ISB knows was the love of Chandler Blake's life. If Juliette tells her story then I might as well call up Headquarters and go naner naner naner , here I am."

Chelsea giggled in spite of herself. "Naner naner naner?"

"Ollie ollie oxen free." He chuckled, seizing on the appearance that her mood had lightened somewhat.

"So, what are you going to do?"

"I don't know.... I'm sorry I hurt you Chelsea..."

"Your superpower?" she smiled sadly, remembering a conversation they had shortly after they met.

"What?"

"The night you showed up at my apartment stoned out of your mind on cocaine, you told me hurting women was your superpower."

"I don't want to hurt you." He had told her that night.

"Then don't hurt me." She was sure it could be, it should be, just that simple.

"I warned you."

"Yeah, you did."

"Chelsea, I want to marry you. I want us to spend the rest of our lives together. I'm not perfect. I've told you that a million times. I'm not perfect. But…." He paused. "When we have babies, I'll just spend the night at the hospital with you… how does that sound?"

Tears welled up in her eyes. "I love you Chandler. I actually do understand how you could have been with someone else during the time we were apart. I do understand that. But what I don't understand, what I can't forgive, is you lying to me. If I can't trust you to tell me the truth then, I can't live with you. You can't lie to me. Not about anything. Not ever again."

"I get that."

"Do you? I hope so because I am serious about this. As serious as I've ever been about anything. I cannot forgive one more lie. I've reached my maximum capacity for that. Not another lie. Not another one. So, right now, if there's anything you haven't told me, anything you've lied to me about… you need to clear it up. Right now, I can't take any more surprises."

Chandler sat down hard, leaned his head back against the

sofa cushion, stared, pensively, at the ceiling and then, shook his head negatively.

"There's nothing Chelsea. I promise."

She walked across the room, sat down in his lap and wrapped her arms around his neck as he buried his head in her shoulder. "OK. So, what are we going to do about Juliette?" Chelsea asked. Part of her, the biggest part of her, was still angry. It would take a while to get over it. Maybe she would never fully get over it. She wasn't sure. But, she rationalized, they were apart, when it happened.

It wasn't like he left her at home to go out and cheat, she told herself. And what were her options? It seemed to her she had two choices. She could forgive him and move on with their lives together, or she could not forgive him. She could leave. Go back to Mississippi and spend the rest of her life alone.

She would never find anyone else she loved the way she loved Chandler. She was convinced of that. Three years without him had left no doubt. He was the love of her life. She couldn't just move on from him. So, in that moment, she made her decision. She chose to forgive him. But the relationship was damaged. Maybe not fatally damaged, but definitely on life-support. It would be a long time before she would fully trust him again… if she would ever fully trust him again.

CHAPTER TWENTY-SIX

"I was so happy to hear from you." Chelsea enthused, as she took a seat by the window that looked out on the water. She was in Starbucks where, at his invitation, she had met Anatole for coffee after work. "I was afraid you were mad at me…."

"Mad? Why?" A puzzled expression crossed Anatole's face as he sat down across from her.

"Mad because… well, I felt kind of weird that night when we were out dancing, and I ended up leaving with Jean-Luc. I mean, I know we were just out as friends but everyone else was with a date, you and I were there, together, and…."

"Don't worry about that. I knew the deal between us. I was surprised, shocked actually. Maybe a little embarrassed. From what you had told me, I didn't really expect you to be hooking up with anyone. I thought you were still in grief over your ex…. the one that died. I worried a little that you might be making a mistake… jumping into something…."

"I know. It was weird. I don't know how to explain it. It had been three years since Chandler died and Jean-Luc was the first guy I met that… you know….” She blushed, unsure of the words to use.

“Charged your batteries?” Anatole suggested, a sly smile on his face.

Chelsea laughed. “Yeah, the first to charge my batteries, and I just went for it.” She had given the same explanation to Charlotte, Miranda, and Chloe already, and it was now so familiar, so easy to her, that she did not even feel the pang of conscience that she had once felt over telling things that were less than true.

“I just thought, ok, I like this guy. He appeals to me. I’m not usually someone who goes home with a guy the night I meet him, but I really felt like I needed to move on…. So, I did.”

“And it worked out for you.”

“Yeah, it did.”

“I’m glad, Chelsea. You seem happy and I’m happy for you.”

“Well, thank you; but I get the feeling there’s a but, coming.”

“No but… not about you being happy. I just feel like I need to tell you something. I’ve felt like I needed to tell you this for a while… and I’m not sure how to broach the subject.”

“I prefer the direct approach.” Chelsea suggested. “Just say what you need to say. She had no idea what he was talking about, but the worried crease in his brow alarmed her.

“Easier said than done. But… ok. I was out a couple of weeks after the night you met Jean-Luc. Met a woman. An incredibly attractive woman. She walked right up to me and asked me to dance. That doesn’t happen a lot. I mean, usually I have to make the first move and then, I’m rejected as often as not. So, this really got my attention. She was hot and she wanted me. We danced, hit it off, and I went home with her. And, just for the record, I'm always the type of guy who will go home with a girl the night I meet her." He winked suggestively.

"Charlotte told me you were dating someone."

"Yeah, I was dating someone."

"Was? Did the two of you break-up or something?"

"Yeah, we did, Chelsea."

"I'm sorry to hear that." She sympathized. "You know, when you're happy in love, you want everyone else to be happy in love. You know?"

"Yeah, well, I didn't say anything about love so..." he laughed. "We had a nice relationship. It was mutually satisfying while it lasted. I'm good with the whole thing, I just thought you needed to know that she was very interested in you and Jean-Luc. Interested in how the two of you met. Actually, after a while, I began to think that maybe she was more interested in getting information than she was in our relationship. I got suspicious that she might be a reporter.... Like the paparazzi or something, so I didn't worry about it. But, when we broke up, we had an argument and she admitted she only hooked up with me to get information about you."

"She wanted to know about me?"

"Yeah, about you and Jean-Luc.... Chelsea, I hate to tell you this. I've struggled with the decision about whether or not I should even mention it. I don't want to cause you and your guy any trouble but when I heard you were engaged.... And that's so out of character for Jean-Luc Moreau. I mean, the man is on the record many times saying he would never marry and..." he paused, obviously hesitant to continue and Chelsea found herself almost hoping he would not. "Chelsea, Juliette, that's the girl's name that I was dating, Juliette thinks Jean-Luc may not be who he claims to be."

Chelsea steeled herself, smile frozen on her face as she hoped her reaction did not show the alarm his words had created in her mind. "What do you mean? Who else would he be?"

"She doesn't know. She thinks that maybe Jean-Luc died in the car wreck and someone assumed his identity."

"Why would anyone do that?"

"Money. I'm sure you know, Jean-Luc is a multi-millionaire. He has no known heirs."

"That's absurd." Chelsea gasped, hoping the panic she was feeling was not evident in her voice

"Well, ok… I don't know the guy. I thought, when I heard the story, it was over the top, but I thought I should warn you anyway. She's sharing this theory with just about anyone that will listen, and she's implicating you in the whole thing."

"Implicating me? How?"

"Well, she says that when she and Jean-Luc were seeing one another, sleeping together, he called her Chelsea on several occasions. Like, maybe he knew you, before the two of you met…. that night at The Emerald Club. Like maybe you're involved in the whole scam. I assured her that wasn't true. I told her that I knew you. She pretended like she didn't know we knew each other, at first, but eventually she confessed. She was in the bar that night, watching Jean-Luc. She saw the two of you leave together. She sought me out, thinking she'd have a sympathetic ear for the story since Jean-Luc stole my date. I explained that we were just friends. I told her your fiancé had died and you came to Istanbul to get over it. I…. uhm…. defended you as much as I could… but she wasn't convinced. Not at all."

"Wow. Well, thank you for defending me and for even

telling me. I really appreciate the support. What a strange story." Chelsea hoped her laughter didn't sound too forced or artificial.

"That's what friends are for." Anatole smiled and the subject was closed. They spent the next hour talking about her job, her wedding plans, a recent trip he had made, back to Moscow. Small talk between friends. But Chelsea's heart was racing, and she was eager to get home to Chandler and tell him what she had been told.

At the end of the evening, Anatole walked her to the sidewalk where, rather than take the subway, she hailed a cab. Inside, she waved goodbye, still smiling at him, but when the cab pulled away, the smile left her face, and she began to shake uncontrollably. This could be real trouble.

CHAPTER TWENTY-SEVEN

"What if she demands a DNA test or something like that?" Chelsea asked, pacing across the floor of the main cabin in their cruiser, as Chandler listened to the story.

"Chelsea, calm down. She has no standing to demand a DNA test."

"Well, who does? And what if she gets to that person? What if she convinces them you're an imposter? What if they demand a DNA test? And you know, it doesn't even matter, actually, whether she gets the DNA test or not, because if she spreads this story around enough, and the ISB gets hold of it, how long do you think it's going to take them to put it altogether and figure out who you really are."

Chandler forced his lips together, exhaling forcibly.

"Ok, you're right there. That is, or at least could be, a problem."

"Exactly. So, what are we going to do?"

"Hope that it doesn't happen."

"Hope that it doesn't happen? What do you mean hope

that it doesn't happen? That's the best you've got. Hope that it doesn't happen? You need to do something to shut her up."

"What can I do?"

"You're too calm about this." She announced, sitting down beside him on the sofa. "What are you thinking? Do you have a plan? Chandler I've told you already… you can't keep things from me, anymore. Tell me what you're going to do. How are you going to handle this? I need to know."

"I don't have any plan. But Chelsea, the thing is…. she has no proof. None whatsoever. She's a disgruntled ex-girlfriend, honestly, I wouldn't even call her a girlfriend. We didn't date. We weren't seen around town together. She popped into my hospital room and we screwed. I honestly don't think anyone ever saw us together. She may have told people, but I doubt if she could even prove that we ever hooked-up. Now, she's sounding-off because the man she's still got a thing for is marrying another woman. Her claims have no credence…. Also, hard as it was, that year and a half we were apart, after I had the surgery, works in favor of the story of Chelsea and Jean-Luc. ISB does not know that I paid off Jean-Luc's debts before I sent for you… they might believe I would have plastic surgery and change my identity so we could be together…. But they would question us staying apart for so long afterward, so that makes the story, our story, far more credible"

Chelsea sighed, beginning to relax. "OK. That makes sense. I guess. But what if the ISB hears the story she's telling and decides to do a DNA test just to make sure. I mean, Chandler, we eat at restaurants, we drink at bars…. It wouldn't be hard to get your DNA from a glass you drank from, a fork you used to eat, if they decided they wanted it. What happens if they check your DNA and… ?"

"I guess we are screwed." Chandler teased, laughing as he spoke.

"It's not funny." Chelsea complained.

"No, it's not. I'm sorry." He agreed, contritely. "But it's also not something I am going to ruin my life, ruin our lives, worrying about. I worked too hard, went through too much for us to be together… so did you. We are free and clear right now. I should not have gotten involved with Juliette. I made a mistake. But there's nothing I can do about that now. I'm just not going to spend the rest of my life worrying about what I'm going to do if the sky falls. I want to enjoy our life together."

"So do I."

"Ok then, stop worrying about Juliette. She's not going to hurt us. I promise you she is not."

"How can you be so sure?"

"Because I am. Stop worrying about it Chelsea."

CHAPTER TWENTY-EIGHT

Days turned into weeks. A huge snowfall hit Istanbul in late February. The city was transformed into a winter wonderland. Chandler and Chelsea made snowmen in almost every park in the city. They went ice skating with Ajax and Charlotte who had reconciled after New Year's Eve, and also recently became engaged. Chelsea marveled at how easily Chandler had become Jean-Luc. But the effortless way that he had slipped into the lie about his identity also concerned her. It wasn't something she had given thought to before, but since she learned about Juliette, she had come to realize, he was an exceptionally good liar.

She watched him, with a grudging admiration, talk nostalgically, with Ajax, about their racing days… memories from four different continents. The night that Jean-Luc had first won a Formula One Championship. The women, there were many… whom they had played with along the way. The memories were not his own, but he was convincing. Too convincing. It was jarring. Something she thought about many nights after he had gone to sleep.

“Who would have ever thought we would end up here, in committed relationships?” Ajax asked.

“Not me.” Chandler conceded with a laugh. “It was definitely not in the ten-year plan.”

“What ten-year plan?” Ajax scoffed. “You were always so fatalistic… we could barely get you to make plans for the weekend on a Wednesday.” He laughed.

“Not really….old friend.” Chandler covered the slight gaffe, quickly. “Truthfully, I always had a plan. I was just too superstitious to share it.”

“Didn’t know that…. but, yeah, I guess it makes sense. The life we were leading, especially, you… the chances you took when you were driving… at some point, I guess we both knew, you were going to end up hitting a wall. It was inevitable”

“I guess we did.” Chandler agreed.

“To good memories.” Ajax clinked his glass of Scotch against Chandler’s.

“To a good future.” Chandler agreed.

With no further contact from Juliette, spring came, and Chelsea began to breathe easier. It seemed they had dodged another bullet. In late May, she resigned and on the final day of the school year, she, and Jean-Luc, met with friends at the Emerald Club for a final party before they returned to the United States.

“I can’t believe you’re leaving us.” Chloe said, forlornly.

“I’ve loved every minute of my life in Istanbul, but I miss the states.” Chelsea replied.

“You’re lucky, Jean-Luc was so willing to go with you.” Miranda said.

“It’s really the best thing I could do for myself….” Chandler explained. “It’s hard to be here, so close to my friends in the racing world and not be able to participate. I need to move on. Start a new life.” He explained.

“And you don’t think you could ever race again?” Miranda’s date, a new guy named Derek, asked.

“Unfortunately no. My doctor said he could never, in good conscience, clear me to go back to racing. I suffered a good deal of brain damage in the wreck. I was blessed in that, it doesn’t affect my normal, everyday life…. But my reflexes are slow. Eye-hand coordination is not at 100% either. Those two issues alone would make me a danger, not only to myself, but to everyone on the track.”

“It’s a real shame. You were truly a gifted driver.” Ajax said. “One of the best I’ve ever seen.”

Chandler nodded. “Thank you.”

“But I guess it is one of those things where we can’t complain too much. Personally, I’m just too glad that you’re alive. Man, I thought you were dead that day.”

Chandler nodded again. This was, he had confided in Chelsea, the comment that was most difficult to live with; the comment which made him cringe. Jean-Luc, Ajax’s friend, was dead. His death had worked out very conveniently for Chandler, but it didn’t change the fact that many people who loved the man, had lost their friend, and been denied their opportunity to grieve. Chandler rarely suffered from an attack of conscience, about anything, but this one bothered him.

The party lasted for several hours…. Drinking, dancing, playing pool, just as they had the night Chelsea first encountered Jean-Luc. Many of their friends from the dock popped in. Several of the teachers from the school were there, as were several of Jean-Luc’s racing buddies. And, shortly before midnight Anatole arrived.

“I was in London on business, but I flew home this

evening when I was done. I had to say goodbye to you and to wish you luck."

"Thank you Anatole. You've been a wonderful friend. I will always appreciate your friendship. You brought me here the night that I met Jean-Luc. I will love you forever for that."

"I feel the same way. And I'm glad you're not angry with me."

"Why would I be angry?"

"For bringing the stories that Juliette, may she rest in peace, told me. I hated doing that, but I felt you needed to know."

"May she rest in peace?" Chelsea repeated his words. "What do you mean by that? Is she dead?"

"You didn't know?"

"Know what?"

"She was murdered several months ago."

Goosebumps broke out on Chelsea's arms. "Murdered? What happened?"

"Apparent robbery." Anatole turned pale as he spoke.. "The weekend after you and I talked, actually. They said she had been out at a club… she left alone, according to witnesses, but she must have met up with someone, afterward. No sign of breaking and entering in her apartment, but she was found, in her bed, the following day. Apparently, someone had held a pillow over her head and suffocated her. Her purse was gone. Maybe some jewelry as well. Friends told the police she wasn't known for carrying copious amounts of money with her, so they wouldn't have got much by taking her wallet, but she had a ruby necklace and earrings that looked to be expensive. She wore them a lot. They didn't find it among her things. So, they assume robbery. No sign of disturbance otherwise."

Chelsea stared at him. Surprise and shock had rendered her silent. She could not think of a single thing to say.

"It was a troubled time for me. Because I was the last man known to be seeing her on a regular basis, the Polis questioned me several times. I was afraid I was going to be charged. Fortunately, my apartment surveillance cameras caught me going in that night about ten, and not going out again. She was still at the club until after midnight, so I was in the clear. Rough time, though."

"I'm--- I'm sorry you went through that." Chelsea swallowed.... hard. Chandler's words... *Don't worry. She's not going to hurt us. It's going to be ok...* running through her mind. He had been so calm. So, resolved.... Shut up! She told herself, as her thoughts went to places she would never consciously allow them to go.

She kept her eyes focused on Anatole, nodded as he spoke, but in her mind, she was in Malibu, California... almost four years earlier. She and Chandler had walked on the beach and he finally confirmed her suspicions... he was an undercover agent.

"Have you ever killed anyone?" she asked as the sun was setting over the Pacific.

"Only when I had to." He answered, a wry smile on his face; so detached from the question, and the answer, that she wasn't sure that he was serious.

"So, you have killed people?"

Chandler was uncomfortable when she repeated the question. "Chelsea, I've never been an assassin. I haven't ever been given an assignment to kill someone. I wouldn't have taken that kind of assignment if they had tried. I am not a killer for hire."

"But...."

"But, if it comes down to them or me.... One of us is

going to die.... Well, I was always determined it wasn't going to be me. I avoided it when possible. I don't like killing people. But...." She could still remember the pained look on his face as he stared out to sea. Sighing deeply, he turned to her and continued.

"I was told by a buddy of mine, in the ISB, that every time you pull the trigger, it's a little easier than the time before. That's not true with me.... It never gets any easier. I value human life. I don't like to take it. But if I have to, if it comes down to a matter of survival, then, yeah, I can do it. I have done it. And I hope I don't ever have to do it again but if I do.... if I find myself backed into a corner... if it comes down to me or them...."

"You'd do it again."

"I have a strong sense of self-preservation."

Chelsea looked across the room at Chandler with his new face... laughing with Ajax and a few of Jean Luc's other racing friends, and a chill went down her body. Had he killed Juliette? Would he have considered that self-preservation?

No. Absolutely not, she thought, trying desperately to push the thought from her mind. But she wasn't sure. She wasn't sure at all. They had been through so much together.........but the trust she once had in him had been damaged, and now, she couldn't say, even to herself, that she was one hundred percent positive he was not capable of murdering someone who posed a threat to his survival.

Would he have considered Juliette that kind of threat? If he did, then, though it broke her heart to admit it, even to herself, she knew he would most definitely have been capable of killing her.

CHAPTER TWENTY-NINE

"Ok...." He said, resignation in his voice, as they walked into the cabin of their boat. "What's wrong?"

"I'm just tired." she replied. It was true. She was tired. And she needed time to process her thoughts.

"No, you're not just tired. Your attitude went south in a big time, very noticeable way, after you danced with Anatole. I'll be glad when we are back in the states and that asshole is out of our lives forever. I'm assuming he had more tales from Juliette; but Chelsea, I don't care what she said... I've told you the whole truth about that situation. I know I was wrong to get involved with her... I know I was wrong to not tell you the truth about the matter to begin with... I've taken my lumps for those things.... But there's nothing else. So, whatever she's told him, that he has chosen to relay to you...."

"She hasn't told him anything, Chandler. She can't tell him anything. She's dead."

She watched his reaction. To her enormous relief, he definitely looked surprised.

"Dead? What do you mean? Dead?"

"Dead. What do you think I mean?"

"You mean like dead, dead. Like no pulse, or heartbeat, dead? What the hell? She was too young to die. What happened? "

"She was murdered, Chandler. Just a few days after Anatole and I had coffee back in the winter, just a few days after he told me about her suspicions, she was murdered."

"Are you sure about that?" the confused expression remained on his face, and Chelsea couldn't help but wonder if he was overplaying his surprise.

"Yeah, I'm sure. I don't think it's something Anatole would lie about. He said he was even questioned by the Polis because they had been dating and broke up just a few weeks before it happened."

Chandler sat down on the sofa, hard. "Well, obviously he wasn't charged, so who did it? What happened?"

"He hasn't been charged, but no charges have been filed. He had an alibi. It's still under investigation. They found her in bed. Someone suffocated her with a pillow. No known motive other than her purse was missing." Chelsea continued, telling Chandler the same story that Anatole had told her.

"I knew I hadn't seen any sign of her in several months. I guess that explains why."

"Were you expecting to see her?"

"Yeah, Chelsea, actually I was. After she approached you on New Year's Eve and then went and dug up your ex-boyfriend…."

"Anatole is not my ex-boyfriend. You're the one who cheated, not me." She snapped.

"OK, sorry, calm down. Why the hell are you so defensive? I'll rephrase…after she seemed to target a guy you knew and told him her theories; I was expecting her to turn up with some sort of blackmail scheme. I expected it for a while, and I was surprised when it didn't happen."

"You haven't seemed very worried about it at all."

"I wasn't worried. I told you I would handle it, if it came up. I was just surprised when it didn't…" Chandler blinked several times as a look of realization spread across his face. "Chelsea, you don't think I had anything to do with her murder, do you?"

She stared steadily into his eyes, desperately wanting to say no and mean it but….

"Damn woman… you think I killed Juliette?"

"No… Not really." Her voice was fraught with uncertainty.

"Dammit. You think I killed her."

"I don't know what to think. You told me… we were at Malibu, walking on the beach…I asked you if you had ever killed anyone and you skirted the issue; but when I pushed it, you said you had never been an assassin but there had been a few times when it was you or them, and when that happened, your self-preservation instinct was strong… those are the words…. You said, your self-preservation instinct is strong. And I said, so you have killed people. And you said, yes, but only when I had no other choice…"

"And you think that was one of these times. Damn. I can't believe you. You actually think I killed Juliette. Chelsea, there were times when I was working for the agency when I came face to face with someone with a gun. They were going to shoot me if I didn't shoot them. I'm still here. That should tell you all you need to know… but, baby, that was a life-or-death situation…. I'm not going to go kill a woman because she has some suspicions…."

"You said you would handle it, no matter what it took,

you promised me she wouldn't hurt us. How could you be so sure of that?"

"I was talking about paying her off. I figured I was about to be blackmailed. I wasn't..." Chandler's expression of shock turned suddenly to anger. "You know what, forget it. I'm not going to stand here and calmly discuss whether or not I killed an ex-lover. If that's what you think of me...." He was interrupted by the jangling of Chelsea's phone. "Who the hell is calling you at two o'clock in the morning?" he growled as she quickly took her phone from her purse.

A puzzled expression crossed her face. "It's your Uncle Doug. Why would he be calling me?"

"I told him to call you if he wanted to contact me... in case anyone was monitoring his phones. You two are close, as far as the world knows, he doesn't know Jean-Luv." He grabbed the phone from her hand. "Doug? What's going on? It's late here and..."

His countenance changed before Chelsea's eyes. His eyes were wide, dark, and suddenly quite moist. His complexion grew pale, his bottom lip trembled and the hand holding the phone shook ever so slightly. She was suddenly frightened. She had seen this reaction once before. The miscarriage. He had walked into the hospital with the same devastated expression on his face.

"Chandler, are you ok?" she asked but she knew the answer to the question. He most definitely was not ok. Something awful had happened... she had no doubt, but what?

"Chandler?" she reached out and touched his hand, but he pulled away. Stood up. Walked to the glass doors of the boat to look out into the dark night.

"Chandler?"

"Yeah, I'm still here." he mumbled into the telephone. His voice was hoarse and emotional. "What happened?"

"No that can't be right… he wouldn't…. no that can't be right, that doesn't even make sense." He closed his eyes, shook his head as if rejecting the news coming from the other end of the call. "Are you sure?" he asked after listening for several moments. "Yeah, I get that? I mean, are you sure it's him? Is it possible there's a mistaken identity or…?"

"OK. Yeah. Ok. We were planning on leaving for New York at the end of the week… but we will change our plans and come on tomorrow. Yeah, definitely. We will be on the first flight out. …. Take care of Mom and Cammie for me. Tell them I'll be there soon. Yeah."

Chandler ended the call, walked back to Chelsea, and handed her the phone.

"Baby what is wrong?" she asked as he sat down, still shaken.

"Chandler, what is wrong?"

He took a deep breath. "My father…." He hesitated and then almost laughed. "I can't say the words. I literally can't say the words."

"Something happened to Isaiah? What happened to him? Is he ok? Chandler, talk to me. Tell me what happened to Isaiah."

"He … he died, Chelsea. He died."

CHAPTER THIRTY

It was four o'clock the following afternoon when they arrived at LAX. Chandler was quiet, reflective for most of the flight. The topic of Juliette's death had been shelved, forgotten. It would not be mentioned, again.

Chelsea understood, intuitively, that the next several days were going to be among the most difficult of his life. The relationship with Isaiah had been fraught with tension since long before she had met Chandler, but she knew there was much love between the son and his father. And, because of the extraordinary nature of his current situation, it was a love, a grief, that he could not show to the world.

As far as most of the world knew, the two men, Isaiah, and Jean-Luc, had never met. Even if someone was privy to the two weeks they had all spent in Amasra, that would have been explained by Chelsea's closeness with the family.... not his. Isaiah Blake had been an immensely popular, long-term United States Senator. There were going to be many people at the funeral... Chelsea had no doubt, and Chandler was going to have to assume a concerned bystander's posture to protect his own identity. He could be there, as her fiancé but, he could not exhibit the overwhelming grief he was suffering. She wasn't at all sure he could pull it off.

Fortunately, his uncle, Doug, had understood the problematic nature of the situation. When they arrived at the oceanside home in Monterey, only the immediate family was present.

"I expected a crowd." Chandler said, as they walked into the drawing room.

"There was one, but I sent them all home when Chelsea texted me that the two of you had arrived at the airport. I knew you needed some time with your mother and sister, and, well, it was time that did not need to be witnessed." Doug explained as they walked into the living room.

Cameron was sitting in an armchair beside the fireplace rocking sleeping baby Chandler, as his mother, Ronnie stood staring out the window into the luscious flower garden.

"Thank God you're here." Ronnie said, as she walked into Chandler's open arms. "Thank God you're here." she repeated as the tears began to flow. "I was thinking about you this morning. I was thinking.... At least Chandler is still alive. At least he is coming back to us. I don't know what I would do if I had lost both of you. This is so hard. I don't know what I would have done if I had lost both of you."

Chandler nodded. The pain he was feeling clearly etched on his face. Mac, Cammie's husband, took the sleeping child from her arms, and she rushed from her chair to enter the family embrace. For a long time, they held each other and cried.

"He was a shitty husband." Ronnie said, finally tearing away from the hug. "A completely shitty husband."

"Mom." Cammie gasped, horrified.

"It's true. I always tried to hide it from you two because, he loved both of you, he loved you with all of his miserable heart, and I didn't want you to know what an asshole he actually was, but he was a shitty husband. I'm not lying to you. Ask Chandler. He knows. I didn't know he knew until after we found out he was still alive. I didn't know he knew… but you did, didn't you? You knew he was a shitty husband."

"Chandler, what is she talking about?"

"It's true, Cammie. He was…well, there were a lot of women. He wasn't a good faithful husband to mom but… Mom, you weren't exactly…"

"I wasn't exactly what? A saint? No, I know, you're right. I had my share of lovers over the years…"

"Mom…." Cammie's eyes grew large.

"I'm sorry baby, but it's true. He was a shitty husband, he cheated on me from the beginning…. I'm almost certain he screwed Betty Carter, one of my bridesmaids, the night before our wedding. That's just who he was… he screwed around, a lot… and one day I thought well hell, if he can have lovers so can I. So, I had an affair. The pool boy. He was outraged. Isaiah, I mean, he was outraged. Threatened to leave me. I said, yeah right, I know you're not ever going to walk away from my family money. So, you're just going to have to put up with me screwing around the same way I put up with you and your whores. He hated it. He was so pissed off. And I loved it. I enjoyed the hell out of the affair, and I enjoyed Isaiah being so pissed off even more. …. So, a few months later, I screwed his press secretary. Drove him crazy. He didn't like it at all, but I said, asshole you're just going to have to deal with it. It always made him so jealous. And I have to tell you, I liked him being jealous. It was the way I knew he loved me. I got to the point that I didn't even care if he screwed around as long as he was discreet about the whole thing… but he hated it when I had a lover. It just drove him crazy." Ronnie laughed bitterly.

"It's how I always knew he loved me. I knew he loved me even though there were so many different women. And I loved him too. I learned to cope with his women by taking my own lovers, but I always loved him. I hope he knew that."

"Chandler did you know…" Cammie asked.

"Yeah, I found out while I was working at the agency…."

"Why didn't you tell me?"

"Because I knew you were going to be devastated…and I didn't want to be the one who did that to you."

Cammie walked back to the chair beside the fireplace and burst into tears as she sat down. "I thought my parents had the perfect marriage…. I did. I thought they had the perfect marriage."

Chandler stared, sympathetically at his sister for a moment; then, turned his attention to Doug who was offering him a crystal glass of amber liquid. "Thanks, I need that." he took a large sip.

"And I need some answers. You wouldn't tell me how this happened on the telephone. Said, wait till I got here. So, I'm here… what the hell happened? Did he have a heart attack or something?"

"It appears he died from an acute overdose of sleeping pills." Doug explained, studying Chandler's expression carefully as he spoke.

"When did Dad start taking sleeping pills?"

"After you err… died…. He took sleeping pills… regularly."

Chandler was ashen. "So, it's my fault?" he sank into a brocade sofa in front of the fireplace. "Damn. What the hell, though? Did he accidentally overdose, or have a reaction? I know he knew better than to mix sleeping pills and alcohol so…. I still don't get it. How did this happen?"

"He left a note." Doug continued.

"What do you mean he left a note? A note about what?"

"He left a typewritten note about why he did it."

"Why he did what?"

"Why he took so many pills."

"Are you trying to tell me he committed suicide?"

"The note said that he had spent three years grieving over your death and he could no longer stand the pain of losing his son, so he was ending it all." He had gotten a refill on his pills the morning before he died, ninety tablets, and the bottle on the floor beside his nightstand was empty. It looks like he took them all.

Chandler groaned, as he leaned against the back of the sofa, tilting his head up toward the ceiling. "I can't believe this."

"Wait a minute." Chelsea said. "That doesn't make any sense…"

Chandler sat up straight, looking first at Chelsea, then Doug, and back to Chelsea. "You're right. That doesn't make any sense. He knows, he knew, I'm not dead. So why would he…"

"I know." Doug said solemnly. "We talked about it last week. He knew you weren't dead. He was quite happy about it… and worried you were going to be mad at him about something he had done, recently."

Chandler groaned. "What had he done? Do I even want to know."

"You're not going to like it."

"Oh shit, what did he do?"

"He had put out some feelers about the ISB? He was conducting a top-secret senate investigation of the organization."

"Dammit. I told him not to do that. I told him how

dangerous that would be." Chandler sprung from his seat, paced across the floor. "Why did he do it?"

"He did it in a way that he thought would protect everyone. He told the committee that he had come into possession of a safety deposit box that belonged to you. Claimed you had information in the box indicating you were in the ISB and he wanted to know more about it. Wanted to know what it was."

Chandler groaned. "Damned idiot got himself killed. I told him. Dammit. I told him he couldn't do this."

"He did listen to you, Chandler. He was worried last week. He said that some information about the investigation had turned up anonymously in the Washington Post. It was veiled, but thinly. The article said that a US senator was investigating the existence of a deep state investigative agency. Not much specific information in the article but he thought if someone knew about the investigation, they probably knew he was spearheading it…and he was worried that…

"He was worried that he was going to get his damned self killed."

"He was worried that he was going to cause you some problems. He wasn't worried at all about himself. He just wanted to tell the world you were still alive… he wanted to tell the world that you were, in his words, a hero… and…"

"And he did exactly what I told him not to do, and the results are exactly what I told him they would be." His voice which had been loud, angry, argumentative suddenly became quiet, resigned. "And he got his damned arrogant ass killed."

Chelsea took Chandler's hand in hers, sat down on the sofa, pulling him down beside her. He resisted for a moment before almost collapsing into her arms. He was shaken, crumpled, heartbroken, and so was she. She had been the one who insisted they tell his parents he was alive. She had pushed for the revelations. When they had discussed it, Chandler had expressed concerns that his father would not be able to keep the secret… and he had been right. Obviously. The guilt weighed heavily in that moment.

"I'm sorry baby. I shouldn't have pushed you to tell him you were alive."

"Don't say that. Don't ever say that." Ronnie insisted. "Finding out Chandler was alive brought him back to life. It brought us all back. You don't know, you'll never know, what we went through when we thought we lost you. We needed you back. We needed you to be alive, so we could be alive, ourselves. Isaiah was a damned fool. He should have listened to you. He should not have stuck his nose into this. He didn't write that note, we all know that, and he didn't commit suicide. We know that. But he's responsible… it's on him… he's the one that is responsible for his death, anyway, because you warned him and he went off, half-cocked and got his damned self killed. It's his fault. Not yours. We needed you back Chandler. We needed you back."

CHAPTER THIRTY-ONE

The media reported the official cause of death as a heart attack. "He had a hard time over the past few years… with the death of his only son." His press secretary explained. "He was just worn down. I think it's fair to say he died of a broken heart."

His funeral was held at the National Cathedral in Washington. The President, himself, spoke of his dedication to his family and to the country.

Chandler did not attend the funeral. The family decided it was the best thing to do under the circumstances. He could have gone with Chelsea, but the chances of him becoming emotional and blowing the identity he had worked so hard to create were not worth the risk, in the opinion of his mother, sister and uncle. He remained at his family home, alone, watching on television and making plans.

The following day, the body was returned to California and was interred beside the grave that people believed belonged to Chandler.

There was a reception after the funeral. Two hundred or

more well-wishers, campaign helpers, and supporters milled about in the Blake family home. Speaking in hushed, whispered voices. Chelsea surreptitiously made a plate from the buffet and carried it up to Chandler who remained in their room.

"I brought you some food." She said, as she walked in, and found him sitting at the desk.

"I missed you." She continued, wrapping her arms around his neck.

"I missed you too. I missed you so much." He moaned as he pulled her into his arms for a deep and passionate kiss. He quickly unzipped her dress, pulling it from her shoulders as he pushed her down on the bed.

"Chandler, wait. I have to go back downstairs. Your mom and Cammie will wonder where I am…"

"Let them wonder. I need you. I need you right now." He cajoled her, as he pulled the dress over her head.

"Chandler…"

"Shhh. I want you… right now. I need you. I need you so much." He groaned as he unfastened her bra and buried his face in her breasts.

The lovemaking was fast, furious and there was something else…. she couldn't put it into words, but she knew what it meant. She had known since the moment Doug had told them how Isaiah died… She knew, and she was strangely resigned to it.

After their passion was spent, she curled in his arms, kissing his chest, his neck, his shoulders. Trying to memorize his body. Trying to memorize the way it felt to be in his arms. They were silent for a prolonged period of time before she finally spoke. "You're leaving me, aren't you?"

He sighed. "I love you. I love you, more than you can even imagine. Chelsea, I love you."

'That's what you always say..." She said, her eyes strangely dry, although her heart was breaking.

"It's the one true thing in my life. I love you."

"But...."

"But, I have to find out who did this to my father.... I was stupid to think I could just walk away and eventually it would all be OK. I cost my father his life. I can't risk that happening with you, or Cammie, or mom, or little Chandler. I have to take care of this. If I don't, if I don't end this, then we can never be happy together. We are always going to be looking over our shoulders."

"That's not true." she argued. "We were happy in Istanbul. We were happy there..."

"Were we? Were we, really?"

"Well, I was.... Maybe you weren't but..."

"You didn't trust me.... A week ago, a week ago today, you accused me of murdering Juliette. Remember that? I do. You weren't happy with me, Chelsea. You didn't trust me. And you could never really be happy with someone you don't trust."

"That's not true... I just.... I just.... Dammit Chandler, that's not fair. "

"No, it's not fair. But it's true. And Chelsea, I don't blame you. We've never had an honest relationship. You didn't know who you were getting involved with, not when we first met. I should not have dragged you into my life.... I just, dammit, I just fell in love with you the minute I met you... and I was selfish.... I should have let you go on, live your life, find happiness with someone who could actually make you happy, someone you could trust... I'm sorry. I can't say I regret it because I can never regret us... but I am sorry that I've made such a mess of your life. And all I can do right now is try to right all the wrongs."

"What are you going to do?"

"I'm going to avenge my father's death. And I'm going to kill King... that was my original assignment. I didn't want to go through with it after I found out his true identity... but I have to. It's the only way I'm ever going to be free. It's the only way we are ever going to have any chance at happiness."

"No." she sat up, pushing him away from her as she did so. Shaking her head vehemently in the process. "No, no, no. You don't get to do that. Not again. You don't get to leave me dangling. You aren't going to leave me and promise to return someday. If you go, if you leave me now... then we are finished. It's over. I'm not going to wait on you. If you leave me again, don't expect me to be here when you come back. You're making a decision here. A life choice. You don't get to come and go at your pleasure. If you leave me, it's over."

"I'm going to do what I have to do, Chelsea. I guess you are going to have to do the same thing."

Chandler said good-bye to his mother, sister and uncle that evening after the funeral guests had left. Chelsea did not come down from their room to say the final good-bye.

"Please don't go." Cammie begged. "I want little Chandler to know her uncle."

"She will never know me, not the real me, unless I settle this." He explained.

"I need my son." Ronnie blinked away tears.

"When I come back, I'll be your son." He promised.

"I don't like what you're doing." Doug told him. "I don't like it at all. But I know you have to do it."

Chandler nodded, glancing up the stairs one final time, hoping against hope that Chelsea would come down to say good-bye. She did not.

"Take care of Chelsea for me, please." He said, sighing, sad but determined, and then he walked out the door, followed by his family who stood on the doorstep until the Uber van disappeared around the curve in the drive.

Chelsea was lying on the bed in the darkened room, a few minutes later, when Cammie knocked on the door.

"He's gone." Cammie said, her voice breaking slightly as she spoke.

Chelsea nodded. It was strange how very calm she was. Almost relieved. He had been right, after all. She would have never admitted it to him, but he was right. She loved Chandler Blake. Not Jean-Luc Moreau. The times they spent alone together, in Istanbul, had been wonderful, but being part of a normal society, she had never felt right. Never felt comfortable. She would never have accused Chandler of murdering an ex-girlfriend, never suspected him, but, even though she knew, rationally, that they were the same person, she wasn't at all sure that Jean-Luc was innocent in what happened to Juliette. She didn't trust him. And without trust, it couldn't work. They had put forth their best effort to live a lie. They had failed.

"I told him I wouldn't wait for him." she said. "I'm sorry Cammie. But I can't do this anymore. I know you love him. I know he's your brother… but I can't go through this again. I can't wait on him. Not this time. I've got to move on with my life. Somehow, I've got to move on."

"I know that. And I don't blame you. Not a bit. Chandler loves you. I know you don't believe that right now, but he really does love you. He just… I don't know what his problem is, but I understand that you need more than he can give. You need someone who will be there for you. All the time. I'll support you in whatever you do. But, Chelsea, no matter what happens, you are always going to be a part of our family. I've lost my brother. So, I need my sister. You're my sister. That's the way I've always thought about you. You're my sister. We are always going to be sisters, no matter what happens. Right?"

"Right." Chelsea agreed as the two embraced and once again Cammie began to cry.

Chelsea did not cry. She would never cry over Chandler Blake, again.

CHAPTER THIRTY-TWO

The mall was packed with last minute shoppers. A choir was singing Jingle Bells near the fountain. It was Christmas Eve.

"You're being a big baby." Six -year- old Chandler Blake told the four-year old boy, as they stood in line at the Santa village in San Francisco.

"I not a baby I just don't wike Santa Claus. And I'm not gonna sit in his lap. Mommy said I didn't have to if I didn't want to and I don't want to. I don't have to do it, do I?" he looked up at Chelsea, his eyes imploring her to agree.

"No, you don't have to if you don't want to, sweetie, but Gramma Ronnie is going to put the picture on the fireplace mantle, and you won't be in it. She'll be super disappointed."

"I don't wike Santa Claus." He complained, stomping his foot angrily. "I don't wike him at all."

"It's your choice." Chelsea promised, giving him a reassuring hug. "But how is Santa going to get you what you want for Christmas if you don't climb up in his lap and ask him?"

"I don't want anything for Christmas… Ronnie can get

me anything I want, anyway. I don't need Santa Claus to get me anything."

"You're such a whiny baby. And Ronnie can't get your gifts from Santa Claus. Those are magic. Everyone knows that Santa gifts are magic, and you can only get them from Santa Claus." Chandler shook her head in disgust. "Why does he have to be such a baby, Aunt Chelsea?"

"I'm not a baby."

"Are too."

"Am not."

"Are too."

"I'll beat you up if you say that again."

"You can't beat me up. You're smaller than me. You're a baby. You can't beat me up."

"Can too."

"Ok, stop arguing. No one is beating any one up. My goodness… that's not the way you're supposed to behave on Christmas Eve. What will Santa think? He won't want to bring you any presents if he hears this." Chelsea reprimanded the two children, lovingly. They had spent the day at the Santa village near the Embarcadero and had planned on getting pictures made there. But Cammie had texted just after lunch advising her that the Santa at the Galleria had a better background for the picture.

Just run by the mall on the way home.

Next year, you take them for their Santa pictures, and I'll stay at home and wrap presents, she thought. But, she knew, by next year she would be eager to spend the day with the two children, again. It was one of her favorite Christmas activities.

"That's not the real Santa, Aunt Chelsea." Chandler explained.

"Is too the real Santa." The young boy disagreed.

"No, it's not. Everyone knows that." Chandler continued. "Santa can't be everywhere, so he sends his elves to pretend to be him at the different malls in the world."

"That's not true...."

"It is too true."

"Stop it." Chelsea cautioned, a stern, but loving tone to her voice. It had been a long day. She had loaded the two children into her car at ten o'clock in the morning. She had hoped they would fall asleep during the two hour drive into San Francisco. They had not. Now, it was after four, and they were tired and contentious. Hopefully, they would fall asleep on the ride home, and maybe sleep through the night. That was the plan, but in the meantime, they needed to stop arguing. Her head was beginning to pound.

The bickering did not stop, though. The argument continued until it was, finally, their turn to visit with Santa, and, after making it clear that it was against his better judgment, the young boy climbed, reluctantly, onto Santa's knee and whispered in his ear. Then, with Chandler on the other knee, he sat, morosely, just long enough for a picture before scrambling out of Santa's lap and running quickly back into Chelsea's arms.

She laughed. It would be a prized family photo in the future, she was sure. The beautiful young girl in her red plaid dress smiling as she displayed her missing front teeth, and the little boy, also dressed in Christmas finery, his eyes narrowed, his lips in an angry pout.

"We are on our way home." Chelsea informed Cammie, after the two children had gone to sleep in the backseat. "Make sure you've got everything put away."

"Yeah...uhm... that's taken care of."

"You got everything wrapped? Really?" Between the two of them they had gone slightly overboard on Santa gifts for the children, and Ronnie, who had gone to Aspen to spend the holidays with her newest boyfriend, had, obviously gone completely out of control. Gifts had arrived from amazon daily for almost three weeks.

"Yeah, uhm, we had some help. Chelsea.... We have company."

"Oh, ok.... I thought we were just going to do family tonight. Did Ronnie come home?"

"No. She's on her way, though. I talked to her this afternoon and she's flying in tonight."

"I thought she was coming in tomorrow morning."

"Yeah, uhm. Well, uhm..." the call began to break-up.

"Hello? Hello?" The line was crackling heavily, and, in the distance, she occasionally caught Cammie's voice, but the static was too heavy to decipher anything she was saying. "Oh, ok, Cammie, I can't hear you but if you can hear me, we'll be home in about an hour. The kids are zonked out. They should sleep well tonight." She laughed as she hung up the phone.

Jingle Bells began to play on the car radio, and she sang along as she drove back toward Monterey.

It was almost dark before she pulled the sleek Mercedes SUV in front of the house. She carefully lifted the young boy into her arms, with Chandler opening her eyes and looking around in confusion.

"Good." Chelsea smiled. "I'm glad you're awake. I was wondering how I was going to get both of you inside."

They walked to the door, hand in hand, with the boy sleeping across Chelsea's shoulder.

Cammie opened the door just as they reached it. "Hi." She said, picking Chandler up from the ground. "Hi." She oddly repeated again. Her eyes wide with apprehension.

"What's going on? You look like you've seen a ghost."

Chelsea laughed just as goosebumps popped out on her arms, and the hairs on her neck stood up in a prickly fashion.

"What's going on?" she asked the question again, this time without a smile. It had been a long time since she had a reaction like this. But she had not forgotten the feeling. Nor what caused it.

"I tried to tell you on the phone."

"I know, I lost my signal outside of St. Luis Obispo. You said we are having company for dinner."

Cammie shook her head affirmatively. "I didn't tell him anything. I thought you needed to be the one to do that."

"What are you talking about? Didn't tell who what?"

"She's talking about me." Chelsea gaze shifted to the tall, handsome man walking into the foyer. She stood quietly for a moment. She knew the voice. It had been five years, but she knew the voice the minute she heard it.

She gave no sign of losing her composure. "You got your face back." She said, calmly, coolly. She was totally in control.

"Not exactly, but I did try. My days as Jean-Luc are long gone." He said with a smile. "Sometimes it's hard to completely undo plastic surgery, but… we did what we could."

She nodded, still, beyond the goosebumps on her arms, showing no reaction. She had never once considered how she would feel if this moment occurred. She had never allowed herself to indulge in that fantasy. But if she had, she would have imagined it to be an emotional moment; joyful maybe, more likely, angry, furious. She felt neither. It was as if someone had turned off her emotions. Completely. She felt nothing.

"Is that Chandler?" he asked Cammie, nodding toward the young girl his sister was holding in her arms.

"Yeah. This is my little girl."

"Not so little anymore… She was just a baby…."

"You've been gone a long time, little brother. She's almost seven years old."

"Yeah, I've been gone a long time… too long." He conceded looking directly at Chelsea.

"What about this little guy? Your son?" he asked his sister.

"No, this one is mine." Chelsea informed him, crisply, and, as she spoke, she instinctively kissed her sleeping son's forehead.

Chandler blinked twice, quickly disguising the disappointment in his eyes, those beautiful green eyes, with a smile.

"Well, he's a good-looking young man."

"I think so." Chelsea smiled in agreement, kissing the sleeping child's forehead again.

"Yeah, well, I think I'm going to take Chandler up and put her in bed. Do you want me to take… him, too?" Cammie asked.

"No, I'll take him up in a few minutes."

"Yeah. Ok, then. I guess I'll just go on upstairs, now. Let the two of you get caught up."

Chelsea nodded, walking on into the living room, and carefully laying her son on the sofa.

"I was glad to hear you were spending Christmas with my family. A little surprised but happy. I actually tried to find you in Violet Springs a few days ago. No one knew for sure what happened to you. They said your parents moved out West a couple of years ago. I was just hoping Mom or Cam would be able to tell me how I could get in touch with you… I'm glad all of you have stayed close."

"We have stayed close." Chelsea confirmed. "Mom and

Dad moved out after…" she nodded at her sleeping son. "After he was born. They wanted to be close to their grand-child. Watch him grow up."

"I see…. so, are they nearby?"

"We live in San Francisco. They are across the bridge in Sausalito." She explained. He nodded, his eyes traveling from her face to the sleeping child. There was a moment of awkward silence before Chelsea asked the obvious question.

"So, not to be nosey, it's really none of my business, but what's going on? You got your face back. Aren't you afraid…"

"I'm not afraid of anything, Chelsea. There's no longer any need to be afraid. It took a long time, but I finally managed to take care of things. No one is after me. I'm not in any danger, and I'm not a danger to anyone else…not anymore."

"Famous last words."

"Not this time."

"You finally got free of the ISB?"

He laughed. "No, not exactly. Actually, I run the ISB, now. I'm the director of operations."

"What?" Chelsea couldn't disguise her surprise.

"Well, if you can't beat 'em…." He smiled wryly. "I couldn't bring it down. I realized that, eventually. It was too big, too powerful. The only thing I could do was take it over. Which I did. I was named Director about four months ago. I'm working to make it more accountable. There's some Congressional oversight, now. It's still a top-secret agency, but it's no longer an entity unto itself. There's going to be some regulation. Some of the people at the Pentagon aren't too happy about the whole thing but, they'll get over it."

Chelsea smiled. "Well, congratulations… I guess. Honestly, Chandler, I have to tell you. I didn't expect that."

"No, neither did I but... it is what it is." He sighed. "I guess we never really know where life may take us... until we get there." He turned his gaze to the sleeping boy, again.

"What about you? Looks like things worked out well for you. Your son is a very nice-looking young man. And you look happy. Or at least you did until you saw me. Don't worry. I'm not going to interfere in your life. You told me you were going to move on. Obviously, you did. I'm glad for you. I really am. You deserve a happy life. And I know you're a wonderful mother. I just hope his father appreciates what an incredible woman you are." He stared at her questioningly.

In that moment she regretted the fact that she had never allowed herself to imagine his return. Perhaps, she thought, if she had indulged in a little fantasy, she would have a better idea of what to say next.

She took a deep breath, trying to formulate the myriad of thoughts rushing around in her brain into some kind of coherent statement, but, before she could come up with the appropriate reply, the young boy lifted his head from the sofa and looked around.

"Mommy.... What's going on?"

"Hey sweetie. We're home. You went to sleep in the backseat... like you always do." Chelsea smiled, kneeling down beside the child. She caressed the back of his head, lovingly.

"Where's Chandler?"

"Aunt Cammie took her to bed."

The young boy looked past Chelsea to the man standing only slightly behind her. "Who is that man?" he whispered as he sat up on the sofa.

Chelsea looked at Chandler, hesitantly.... "Uhh, that's uh... well, that's an old friend of Mommy's."

"What's his name? What's your name?"

Chandler stepped forward and knelt down by the child. “My name is Chandler.”

“Chandler? Your name is Chandler? Really? That’s my cousin’s name. Do you know Chandler Blake Scott? She’s a know it all and a brat and she bosses me around all the time.”

“Baby.” Chelsea’s tone was slightly chiding.

“Mommy you know it’s true. She says I’m a brat, but she’s the real brat. But she’s also my best friend. But don’t tell anyone I said that. Boys aren’t supposed to be best friends with girls. Do you know my cousin Chandler?”

“Your cousin?” Chandler turned to Chelsea, a puzzled expression on his face.

Chelsea raised her eyebrows, as she exhaled, forcibly.

“I don’t understand.” He turned back and looked at the young child who he suddenly realized bore a striking resemblance to his sister Cammie, and her daughter. “What’s your name young man?”

“I’m Shiloh.”

“Shiloh?” Chandler choked on the word. His throat had become dry and it felt as if his heart were suddenly beating in cut time. “Your name is Shiloh? His name is Shiloh?” he turned to Chelsea.

She nodded.

“Shiloh Chandler Blake. I go by Shiloh because Chandler got the name Chandler first, because she was born first. She was named after my daddy. Cause her mommy is his sister. And I was named after him too… Chandler was his real name, but Shiloh was his nickname.” He paused, thoughtfully.

“Are you named after my daddy, too?” he asked innocently.

“Chelsea?” Chandler asked, his voice soft, hoarse with emotion.

"Actually baby…" Chelsea began, unsure of the words she needed to speak.

"Wait a minute… you actually look like my daddy. Gramma Ronnie has a picture on the table beside her bed. He has green eyes just like you do. Just like I do, too." Shiloh's eyes growing wide with excitement. The young boy turned to his mother, suddenly shy, he wrapped his arm around her shoulder and whispered in her ear. "Mommy, is that my daddy?"

Chelsea nodded.

"You're my daddy?"

"Chelsea? What do I…? I don't know what to….? What do I…?"

"As a matter of fact," Chelsea blinked back the first tears that had moistened her eyes since the night the doctor had put the screaming baby boy in her arms. "Yes, baby. This is your daddy. He's the Chandler you and Chandler are named for, and he's home for Christmas."

"You're my daddy? Really?"

"Yeah, I'm your daddy." The words felt strange, foreign, but oh so wonderful, as they tripped across his tongue. His hand was trembling as he reached out and stroked the young man's head. "I'm your dad. Hi Shiloh, it's nice to meet you."

"I knew it. Gramma Ronnie always said that you'd be back someday." He studied Chandler's face carefully. He leaned forward and whispered, conspiratorially. "We prayed that you would come back every time Gramma Ronnie read me a story at bedtime… But don't tell Mommy. Ronnie said it would make her mad." Chandler glanced at Chelsea and smiled.

"Grandma Ronnie was probably right about that."

Shiloh studied his father's face for several minutes and then, his mouth dropped open. "Mommy, Chandler was wrong. I can't wait to tell her she was wrong. That really was the real Santa at the mall today."

"You think so?"

"I know so. It had to be… I know it, because today when he asked me what I wanted for Christmas, I told him I wanted him to bring my daddy back and he did. He must have been the real Santa. He had to be."

Chandler could hardly take his eyes off his newly discovered son, but he turned to Chelsea. He had a question and it had to be asked face-to-face.

"You're not married?"

"No, Chandler. I'm not married." Chelsea replied.

"I just assumed… you said you weren't going to wait… you had the son… I just assumed…"

"I didn't wait, Chandler. I've been busy raising my son. I didn't wait on you. I just didn't really have time to move on to anyone else."

Chandler laughed. Not a derisive laugh but a laugh full of relief. A laugh full of joy. A laugh full of hope. He had never imagined that a young son would be waiting for him, but over the years he had, himself, prayed, many times, that Chelsea would be there, when he finally came home.

"You're not going to leave again?" Shiloh asked, as he jumped from the sofa. "Are you?"

"No. I'm not going anywhere." Chandler promised.

"Good. I've got to go tell Chandler that my daddy is here. So, you just wait right here. Don't move. Stay exactly where you are. Don't move. Stay right there. I will bring her down and you can meet her."

"I'd like that." Chandler watched in awe, as his son ran from the room and headed up the stairs.

"Chelsea, I don't know what to say…."

"There's nothing you can say."

"When I left… did you know?"

"No. I found out I was pregnant about three weeks later."

"You didn't have any problems this time?"

"No. It was an easy pregnancy. An easy birth. Your mom and Cammie were with me when he was born. Your mother said he looked just like you, when you were little. And sometimes he does things. It is weird. He turns his head to the side, or he scrunches up his face when he's upset, and it's like looking at a small version of you. Not the resemblance, but the mannerisms. He's little Chandler. Kind of hard to move on when a miniature you is right in front of me every day."

"Thank you." He said, humbly.

"My pleasure. I mean that sincerely. He is the joy of my life."

"I never stopped thinking about you, Chelsea."

"Chandler, please. Don't!"

"I'm sorry, but it's true. I know I'm the worst thing that ever happened to your life, but you are still the best thing…. You and that little boy really are the best things that ever happened to me. I never stopped loving you. I know you don't believe that, but I never stopped loving you."

Chelsea rolled her eyes, annoyed, more by the tumultuous emotions she was feeling than his words. Could she give him another chance? Could she stand another heartbreak? "You're not the worst thing that ever happened in my life. Without you, I wouldn't have Shiloh. You're not the worst thing that ever happened. Not even close." She admitted, reluctantly.

"Oh, baby." He gently caressed her cheek with his hand and leaned in for a kiss, but she quickly pulled away.

"Chandler, damn. You can't just come home after five years and expect me to be waiting with open arms. Whatever I may still feel for you, I'm not completely stupid. I know you could leave me tomorrow and not look back for another five years or longer. ”

“I didn’t expect you to be waiting at all. And I’m sorry. I hoped for it, but I didn’t expect it. And I didn’t expect a son. I’m just kind of overwhelmed right now. But no, of course not. I know you have reservations. I understand that. And, I know you must have questions but…”

“You’re damn right I do. Lots of questions.”

“I’ll tell you anything you want to know. I’m just….” He laughed. “I’m just so happy that you’re here, and you want answers. I thought you probably wrote me off a long time ago and….”

“Maybe I did…” she answered.

“And maybe you didn’t.”

She sighed. “Maybe I didn’t. Not completely. How could I look into that little face and…?” she didn’t finish what she was saying because at that moment, Shiloh and Chandler came rushing down the stairs.

“See. I told you. It’s my daddy. He’s home. I told you. See. Santa brought him.” Shiloh announced.

Chandler eyed her uncle suspiciously. “Are you really his daddy?”

“Yes, I am.” Chandler smiled as he spoke and his smile got even bigger when, to his surprise, Shiloh rushed toward him, wrapping his arms around his neck, in the biggest hug a four-year-old could give.

“I’m so glad you’re finally home.” the young boy said, as he planted kisses on his father’s face. “Gramma Ronnie says you like to ride horses like me and her do. Maybe we can go riding sometime? Do you think we could? I can ride Sophocles all by myself. I ride on the same horse with Ronnie, sometimes. And sometimes she walks and leads Sophocles around and lets me ride by myself. Sophocles is an older horse, so he's gentle. Chandler learned to ride on him too. Now she can ride a big horse and she's learning to jump fences." Once again, he leaned in close to his father's ear. "Don't tell mommy but sometimes Ronnie jumps a fence when I'm riding with her. I'm going to get to jump fences by myself when I'm older but now I have to do it with Ronnie, or just ride Sophocles."

"I remember Sophocles."

"I know. Gramma Ronnie told me you rode him when he was young. Grown-ups don't ride him anymore because he's so old. But he likes for me and Chandler to ride him. Do you think maybe we can go riding together?"

"I can't think of anything in the world I'd rather do."

"And I like to play soccer. Uncle Mac is my coach. Maybe you can be my coach too."

Chandler laughed. "Well, I don't really know that much about soccer."

"That's ok. My daddy will teach you." Chandler piped in. "He taught me how to play. He taught Shiloh, too. He won't mind showing you how to do it."

"Do you want Uncle Mac to teach you how to play soccer?" Shiloh asked, very solemn. The answer to the question was extremely important to him. He loved soccer.

"I'd love for Uncle Mac to teach me how to play soccer."

Shiloh wrapped his arms around his father's neck, squeezing him tightly. "I'm so glad you're home. We're going to have so much fun."

"I'm glad I am home, too." Chandler smiled at Chelsea.

"Me, too." Young Chandler said, as she too, ran across the room, throwing her arms around her uncle's neck.

"Me, too." Cammie said, following her daughter into the room.

Chandler gave his sister a caustic look. "I spent the afternoon with you. You couldn't have given me a little hint."

"Nope. Wasn't my surprise to share." She answered. "You were all worried when I told you Chelsea would be here. Afraid she would be surprised, upset. Not the way you wanted to spring your return on her. And I was thinking, oh boy, you don't even know what a surprise is." She laughed. "But I am glad you're home, little brother. We missed you."

"What about you, mommy? Aren't you glad my daddy's home too?" Shiloh asked.

Chelsea took a deep breath. "Of course, I am…" she reassured her son.

"Then say it."

"What do you want me to say?"

"Say you're happy my daddy is home."

Chelsea nodded indulgently at her son. "I'm very glad your daddy is home."

It was forced. Chandler understood it was more for her son than for him. But the words caused a warm glow to spread through his body as he embraced his son and niece. He had spent five years dreaming of the moment when he could come home. He had hoped and prayed that he would somehow be able to recapture his life, all the while, telling himself that she would probably be forever out of his reach. Somehow, it now seemed, he might have one more chance.

It would take some time. He knew her well. She was determined to be strong. She wasn't going to make it easy on him. But she was here. And they shared this remarkable young boy. His son.

The love was still there, he could see it in her eyes… and they now had a bond that could not be broken. When she realized he wouldn't be leaving again, when she realized he was finally free to love her, and their child… she would give him another chance, he was sure of it. And this time he would not let her down.

The End

It was a long journey, but Chandler finally made it home to the love of his life and their son. But where has he been? What did he do during his lost years? Why is he so certain that he can now, finally, move on with his life? Look for *Chandler Blake: The Lost Years…* coming in the Fall of 2021.

www.ingramcontent.com/pod-product-compliance
Lightning Source LLC
LaVergne TN
LVHW012046160826
845678LV00014B/2723

* 9 7 9 8 7 0 2 9 4 5 3 7 8 *